THE IBEX TROPHY

JOHN CAMMALLERI

AND

SALVATORE CAMMALLERI

iUniverse, Inc.
Bloomington

The Ibex Trophy

iUniverse books may be ordered through booksellers or by contacting:

iUniverse
1663 Liberty Drive
Bloomington, IN 47403
www.iuniverse.com
1-800-Authors (1-800-288-4677)

ISBN: 978-1-4620-2625-8 (sc)
ISBN: 978-1-4620-2626-5 (ebook)
ISBN: 978-1-4620-2627-2 (dj)

Printed in the United States of America

iUniverse rev. date: 6/14/2011

To Mom, from both of us

Author's Note

Notebooks and pens could be found everywhere—the living room, kitchen countertops, my father's den. Some pages would have only a single word written on them; some a phrase; some a sentence. Occasionally my father would compile them, trying to piece together a paragraph or possibly a chapter. There was a novel in him that was trying to come out, and for over forty years he painstakingly worked at it while simultaneously running a business and, with my mother, raising two children.

Born in Italy and having a limited education, my father took a correspondence course in writing to learn some techniques. But the actual writing came in fits and starts, and even when he retired and my sister and I were grown, it seemed as if his dream had left him. Toward the end of the 1990s, when he was in his late seventies, I gave him an old computer and printer that I had replaced. After some quick lessons on using them and the word processing software, he had a better means of writing than he'd had with a pen and paper. The inspiration returned. He completed his novel, although the only editing he was willing to accept was correction of any spelling or grammatical errors, with which he asked me to help. He refused the idea of a professional book editor or anyone, including me, making any suggestions, because he wanted the story told his way. Dad was a bit stubborn, and besides, he had two main intentions, which he satisfied with the publication—first, just to be able to say he did it; second, to set the record straight on the performance of the Italian army during the episode described in the book. He knew it firsthand; he was there. So, in 2000, at seventy-eight, his book was self-published with the title *About Face*. There was never any intention to build a market for his book, and ultimately, he simply gave copies away to family and friends.

My father died in 2003. In 2007 I took an early retirement and became a writer myself, publishing *Protecting the Cittern* in 2010. As I put the finishing touches on that book and contemplated what my next project would be, *About Face* came to mind. I always thought the story was good and, with some editing, could develop a wider audience than my father ever imagined. Having gained some experience and being a member of several writing groups, I decided to rework the novel and place it under the scrutiny of the talented authors in those groups. I then worked with the editors at iUniverse to polish it as much as possible. The result is *The Ibex Trophy*.

My father created the basic story and characters. I changed a few plot points and rewrote much of it to reflect my own style, but in the end, I simply retold it in a way that I hope will bring him the recognition he deserves. I'm proud to share the author's credit with him.

John Cammalleri
June 2011

Credits and Acknowledgments

Excerpts of this novel have been taken from the book *Le Truppe Italiane in Corsica* (Tipografia Scuola A.U.C., Lecce, 1952), with a written permission from its author, General Giovanni Magli.

Portions of this book were originally published as *About Face* by Salvatore Cammalleri.

When first published, Salvatore Cammalleri dedicated his novel to the memory of his 637 comrades-in-arms who, with valor and complete dedication to their duty, tenaciously fought and gave their lives in the bloody battles to free Corsica from the preponderant occupation forces of the German army that took place from September 8, 1943, to October 4, 1943.

Salvatore Cammalleri gave credit and thanks to General Giovanni Magli, who against all odds, conducted himself with honor and dignity in his effort to renew some respectability for the Italian army and to build a base for the destiny of the battered country.

John Cammalleri would like to thank the members of the Morningside Writers' Group, Prudy Taylor Board, and his editors Elizabeth Day and Marna Poole for their valuable input during the writing of this revised novel.

1 *Arrival in Corsica*

"Crespi, I need you in my cabin—now!" Captain Benelli's raspy voice startled Renzo Crespi, a twenty-year-old private, as he peered over the railing of the ship, watching the activity on the docks below.

Renzo never expected to see Corsica, never had any desire to leave his hometown of Agrigento, Sicily. The war changed his plans, as it did for so many young men around the world. The Italian army took him from his premedical studies in January 1942, and he was eventually assigned as an infirmary overseer of a light artillery company. It was part of the two army divisions, the Friuly and the Cremona, which were sent to occupy Corsica, along with other branches of the Italian military. Eighty-five thousand Italian troops were sent to an island with fewer than three hundred thousand inhabitants.

On the night of November 10, 1942, he sailed with his fellow soldiers from the port of Livorno, Italy, aboard one of the vessels that formed an impressive flotilla of transport ships and warships under the command of Admiral Vittorio Tur. The seventy-mile crossing had been safe and uneventful, except for the billowy waves that battered some of the men to intense seasickness all night long.

Until then, Corsica had just been a name on a map for the lanky young soldier, having no special distinction to him beyond its being Napoleon's birthplace. When morning came, they were safely anchored at the Port of Bastia. Renzo was on deck, along with many other soldiers, observing what awaited them. The port itself, filthy and smelly, was antiquated and congested. A large part of the

1

pier was covered with donkey and horse dung. The smell from that, combined with the stench of dead fish floating above oil spills, the fumes of their ships' engines, and the foul odor of rotten seaweed, contributed to the nausea of several of the young men, who needed to go back below to vomit.

Renzo scanned what lay before him. Tall trees, leaves aflame with color under the bright morning sun, bordered a large square bustling with activity. A network of crooked streets and alleyways stretched mazelike from the square as far as he could see. They were lined with apartment houses, shops, and government buildings, many covered in faded and peeling blue, green, or red paint.

From the far side of the square, a church stared down on him. It was an impressive Baroque structure, with double towers outstretched to a blue sky. It seemed that it couldn't care less about the shipload of soldiers who still were unsure as to what their mission was all about. The church bells were silent, and its clock on the northern tower was no help to the villagers who wanted to know the time—the hour hand was missing. The huge white stone cross in the center of the church's triangular roof was the only thing that gave Renzo some comfort—it was as if it were an indication of a silent welcome from God. Renzo was a devout Catholic, and it made him slightly more at ease in a strange and potentially dangerous land.

Renzo's visual exploration was abruptly ended when Benelli called his name—Captain Giancarlo Maria Francesco Benelli wanted to see him immediately. As pretentious as the captain's name sounded, it was legitimate, exactly as it appeared on his birth certificate, and it was how he referred to himself. His soldiers, however, had a shorter name for him. Because of the captain's peculiar raspy voice, which sounded as if he had a handful of sardines perpetually stuck in his throat, they called him *il rospo*, the bullfrog. He was a career man; a balding, paunchy, bachelor of fifty; the only son of a wealthy Fascist family who boasted close ties with the Italian nobility. He liked to wear a monocle most of the time—he didn't need it for his vision, but he believed it made him look more intelligent and sophisticated.

By the time Renzo entered Benelli's cabin, the door of which had been left open, the captain was staring out the porthole with clenched fists on his waist, looking like a Roman centurion. The click of the door's latch as Renzo closed it made Benelli turn around wild and fast.

"My back is killing me," he growled. "Do you have the camphorated oil with you? I need a rubdown."

"No, sir," Renzo answered, standing at attention. "Everything is in the ambulance, and the ambulance is stored in the hull with all the other vehicles." The captain's unexpected and strange request puzzled Renzo. He could not conceive how the only thing his commanding officer was thinking about at this time was the need to relieve his chronic backache.

With a reassuring smile, the captain took a half-empty bottle of camphorated oil from a pocket of his small knapsack. "I didn't think you would. Here," he said, tossing the bottle to Renzo. "We have plenty of time."

"Aren't we going to disembark soon?" Renzo asked.

"Not for a while," the captain said with a shrug. "Admiral Tur and Colonel Farina have gone ashore with a delegation to negotiate the terms of our occupation with the French authorities." He looked out of the porthole once more and snapped, "Come on now! Let's get going." He began to peel off all the paraphernalia he wore. The binoculars were first, followed by the German cameras that always hung from his neck. He then removed a leather pouch containing charts and maps. The black leather belt on which his pistol was securely clipped came after that and lastly, his upper garments, which he deposited with meticulous care on the mate's bunk bed. Finally, bare-chested, he straddled a massive maple chair, his pudgy hands gripping the backrest and his head resting on his crossed arms, leaving a meaty torso half-covered with coiled black hair exposed to Renzo.

Renzo began his work, as he had many times before. He was used to these requests: the captain's backache was an ongoing torment, and Renzo was happy to give his captain some relief and put him in a good mood. Benelli obviously was disappointed because all the rigorous training on beachhead maneuvers that the company had gone through in the past few months was for naught.

One of the captain's many desires was to be able to show off his gallant heroism in action, as he'd told Renzo during previous sessions. Benelli opened up to Renzo often—his tensions disappeared with the comforting massages, along with any discretion. He wished to be given, at least once, he'd said, the opportunity to lead his company onto a battlefield so he could prove his indomitable courage and draw the attention of General Headquarters regarding his wide knowledge of warfare technique, which would guarantee him a promotion to major. Regrettably, his skills would not be needed now, and he was infuriated. As the captain ranted this time, Renzo felt he was facing an eruption of Mount Etna.

"We're an elite company in a strong regiment, one of the best in the nation," the captain continued as Renzo firmly kneaded the muscles in his back, "as good as any of Germany's men. We're well armed, physically and psychologically prepared, and ready and willing to sacrifice everything and to take any risk."

"Yes, sir."

The captain cleared his throat and then, lowering his voice, confided to Renzo, "This Corsican mission is folly. We should be put to better use, but who will listen? There was no good reason to change things."

The captain, now somewhat relaxed and comfortable with venting in Renzo's presence, laid out his thesis on the proper methods of warfare. "We should have proceeded with a nocturnal attack on Malta, as was originally planned. But Il Duce's generals thought it would be too risky—'too many fatalities,' they said—so he changed his mind, just like that." Benelli snapped his fingers for emphasis.

"How did they arrive at that conclusion, Captain?"

"Oh, they cited a few reasons that apparently were compelling enough for Mussolini. Allied troops in North Africa were advancing in Malta daily, driving the Germans out to sea. I admit, Corsica is in an important geographical strategic position, and Mussolini recognized that the island constituted an appealing location for the British. He feared that Corsica, together with Malta and Sicily, could be a logical stepping-stone in the liberation of France and an assault on Europe. This made him want to beat the Allies to the punch so, with that in mind, he telephoned Admiral Tur and ordered him to occupy Corsica immediately. Tur protested, as he should have," the captain continued. "He told Mussolini that it would be extremely difficult, if not impossible, to coordinate a mission of that magnitude on such short notice."

"Did the admiral tell Mussolini why he felt that way?" Renzo asked, pouring more oil onto the captain's back.

"Of course. His reasons were simple. For one thing, you remember the four straight days of steady rain we endured in the mosquito-infested pinelands of Piombino, which made a quagmire of mud out of our camp? He said this would slow down the gathering of troops and equipment. To further complicate matters, the region was in a state of aerial alarm, so everything would have to be executed in complete darkness, for fear of British bombing. This, of course, would endanger the safety of the troops, even though the success of the mission couldn't be guaranteed. The admiral said he needed more time, but Mussolini accepts no excuses. Tur knows the Fascist motto, 'The leader is always right,' and knew that he had no choice. From what I heard, Mussolini furiously shouted, 'I said, immediately!' and slammed the telephone down."

Captain Benelli's detailed revelation of what likely was an extremely delicate military secret completely fascinated Renzo. In silence, he continued with the rubdown, no longer aware of the awful stench of camphorated oil. He could feel anger emanating from each vein in the captain's neck as he spoke. Renzo had seen the captain in this state of nervousness many times, mostly when things didn't go his way. Renzo wanted to try to ease the captain's troubled mind but didn't know exactly what to say. A long pause followed but finally, hesitantly and with much respect, he dared to say, "Is it possible that Mussolini is right, sir? If Corsica is so valuable and so important to the British, doesn't it make sense that it could be just as important to us?"

"No, impossible!" the captain snapped with unrestrained scorn. "There is nothing here that's worth my spit. This is nothing but a hellhole! Just a chunk of wild land filled with uncivilized, savage bandits," he concluded, springing up from the chair. Apparently, he'd had enough of the rubdown. He began to dress, and then, as Renzo hoped, a loud sneeze resonated in the cabin. That sneeze pleased Renzo very much.

Captain Giancarlo Maria Francesco Benelli always sneezed

involuntarily at the end of any event that gave him some enjoyment. He sneezed with satisfaction after a good-tasting meal. He sneezed at the end of a fast ride on the sidecar of a motorcycle, the speed exhilarating him. He sneezed at the conclusion of his frequent pep talks and even at the end of each of Renzo's backrubs. The number and the intensity of the sneezes indicated the degree of his happiness.

"What's going to happen now?" Renzo asked. "What are we to do?"

"Just sit and wait for the admiral's and the colonel's orders," the captain replied, closing his eyes halfway and shrugging his shoulders as if he had lost all his enthusiasm.

****

Their orders came quickly. Within the hour, Tur, Farina, and their delegation returned and immediately summoned all commanding officers to be briefed on their meeting with the French military authorities. Tur explained that the meeting with his French counterpart had been cordial, yet although it was based on mutual respect, the atmosphere had remained restrained and awkward. Admiral Tur understood the meaning of defeat. He knew quite well how humiliating and difficult it was for a soldier, any soldier worth his salt, to lay down his arms and relinquish the rein of command to the conquering enemy without a fight. It is a matter of pride, honor, and patriotism. In such a case, castration would have been preferable, but the French officer had no choice. Under the armistice treaty of June 24, 1940, Italy and Germany had the right to occupy, at will, any French area, including Corsica. So, with reluctance, permission to disembark was granted. However, the French officer warned the Italian commission that even though there wouldn't be any military opposition, he was not to be made responsible for civilian unrest or vandalism.

****

The operation got underway exactly as if it were one of their many drills. Quickly, the wharves were swarming with soldiers. The regiment of infantry came ashore on the sandy beach, while others disembarked on long planks or retractable ladders onto the cliffs of the rocky coast nearby. Armored cars, heavy weaponry, the light artillery, all vehicles including the ambulance, mortars, and mules descended on the banks near the wharves.

Soon after, a sea of boastful soldiers flooded the plaza, and immediately, in perfect order, the convoy lined up. Six heavy half-tracks with a cannon hooked on each were followed by another heavy truck containing the kitchen equipment. Renzo came next, with the ambulance, while a military police motorcycle escort brought up the rear.

Once again Renzo had a chance to admire the contrasting aspects of the town. There, on a majestic pedestal, fanned by the windswept long branches of large palm trees, stood a magnificent statue of Napoleon, who, surprisingly to Renzo, was dressed in the uniform of a Roman emperor. Men with somber, scowling, creased faces, their heads covered by black berets or fishermen's hats, silently lined the sidewalks on both sides of the streets. In a house across the street, he saw a woman with a black kerchief covering her head and tied in a knot under her wrinkled chin. She had a solemn, unsmiling face as she opened the shutters of her window halfway to hang freshly washed clothes on a rope attached to a big hook. Other women had hung their undergarments on long bamboo canes that were anchored like flagpoles on the windowsills. Some stores had placed large black ribbons across their doors as a sign of national mourning.

As Renzo noticed the citizens' demeanor, he tried to imagine himself in their situation—their land now overrun by enemy soldiers. He had conflicting thoughts, believing the Italian mission in Corsica was necessary yet empathizing with the Corsicans' loss of self-determination.

∗∗∗∗

Singing military songs, the soldiers left the port that afternoon, happy that not a shot had been fired and no one had been hurt. They sat on heavy wooden planks anchored across the sides of the trucks, thirty men on each. Lieutenant Vittorio Semprefedele, the senior officer, was in the first truck. Lieutenant Orazio Boschetto was in the second, followed by Second Lieutenant Michelangelo Maniscalco. Captain

Benelli led the convoy in the sidecar of his two-cylinder Gilera motorcycle.

The roadside leading out of Bastia was covered with a series of rubbish heaps. Discarded old tires; empty crates; abandoned, rusted automobiles; and half-rotten lumber piled up along the side streets.

Although not a surprise to the captain and his company, Renzo felt it was unfortunate that the first reaction of the population was negative. At one point, as the trucks thundered up the hill on the outskirts of town, Renzo saw a woman's arm extend from a half-opened window on the second floor of an apartment house. She held a one-handled white vase, and she dumped out its yellowish liquid as their trucks rolled by, accompanying her action with a loud litany of curses. They all knew what that liquid was and, fortunately, it largely missed its target.

The men managed to restrain from reacting to this regrettable form of disapproval—their training included avoiding unnecessary confrontations with the population, and the elderly woman posed no real threat. Fortunately, they continued on with no other incident. Once they crossed the city limits, they crept up slowly and carefully on an endless serpentine dirt road through miles of barren countryside. The bumpy, dusty road was just wide enough to accommodate the large trucks. After three hours of steady, slow climbing they reached their destination, a small village strategically located along the eastern coast of Cape Corse, Corsica's northern peninsula. It was chosen for its proximity to the cities of Bastia and St. Florent, opposite each other at the base of the narrow peninsula, as well as Macinaggio in its northernmost tip.

Night had already fallen, and there was no sign of human life. Only the chilly mountain air greeted them. They exited the vehicles and formed a large circle, several men deep, around the captain. Benelli motioned the 147 men in his company to come as near to him as possible, so he didn't have to speak any louder than necessary.

"Corsica is in a state of alarm. A radio appeal in the name of France, asking for calm and cooperation, had been made jointly by a French officer and Admiral Tur. Apparently, there is no electricity in this village, and for fear of provoking the villagers, we have been ordered to eliminate any loud or sudden noises." The captain folded his hands behind his back and paced as he continued. "Our task in Corsica is clear. We are here solely to protect the island against external attacks. We will not get involved in any internal affairs unless the island's security is threatened. You must keep that in mind at all times while we are here." With that admonition, he dismissed his men.

One-third of the company was assigned to sentry duty. The rest slept sitting on the wooden planks. Assured and confident of the safety provided by their watchful guards, they settled for the night.

Using stretchers as beds, Captain Benelli and Renzo slept in the ambulance. The night was still and peaceful. From time to time, only the lament of an owl, the distant barking of a dog, or the snoring of Captain Benelli interrupted the silence.

2   *First Impressions*

The following morning, Renzo and the rest of the company were comforted to know that in this village no one would attempt to douse the troops with urine from the upper floor of some apartment house, as the old woman had tried to do in Bastia. There were no tall buildings anywhere.

The night before, they had parked their trucks at the edge of a steep cliff overlooking the sea but couldn't get a full appreciation of their surroundings in the dark. Renzo and several other men had some time in the early morning to take in the area. Renzo gazed down on a sleepy little fishing village, where a calm blue sea met a wide horseshoe-shaped beach.

Countless small boats were docked at a natural harbor. Some were turned to one side on the sandy beach, and others bobbed lazily on the mirror-like water, unconcerned that the Italians had come, their colorful sails rolled up on deck. The entire coast looked a picture of tranquility, not a place under siege.

The mountains surrounding the harbor were filled with what appeared from the distance to be fruit trees. Red slate-roofed houses in pastel colors, each with a tiny garden of its own, were grouped neatly in separate clusters in the village. For a short time, Renzo almost forgot where he was—and why. His reverie ended when the raspy voice of Captain Benelli startled him once again and at the same time scared the robins in the trees, making them fly away.

"What the hell are you men doing?" Benelli yelled. "Come on, now! You look like a bunch of tourists. This is a siege, not a pleasure tour. There is work to be done."

The captain was grumpy, and Renzo had a good idea why. His back was probably killing him. He knew the captain craved his daily backrub but there was no time, and certainly this wasn't the place for it. There were too many other things yet to be done. They had to take charge of their positions; they needed to install the communication system with the rest of the regiment and perform many other logistic preparations. Renzo's first job was to distribute the malaria-preventive quinine pills to the troops. The backrub would have to wait.

****

Later that day, as he stood near the ambulance, Renzo poured some water from his canteen into the captain's cupped hands to wash his face. The captain's shirtsleeves were rolled up and his shirt unbuttoned, but he wore his hat to protect his pale, thin-haired head from the sun. Captain Benelli's orderly, Nino Conti, stood nearby, watching impassively.

Nino was a beekeeper from the hills of Calabria who could neither read nor write. He had entrusted Renzo with the delicate mission of reading his mail to him and of writing letters to his mother and his bride-to-be, who were also illiterate and needed a friend to read the correspondence. Renzo enjoyed just trying to put into a logical sequence of words what Nino told him with great passion, accompanied with various hand gestures and eye expressions. Nino followed Renzo's every move until he signed the letter. It was then, with a wistful sigh and unabashed pride, that he would carefully add two big X's—his first and last names—to the bottom of the page.

The trio heard the sound of bells coming from around the bend in the road. A flock of sheep, controlled by two large barking dogs, approached from the west side of the hill and advanced noisily toward them in a cloud of dust. Behind them, an old man sat sideways on the bare back of a gray donkey. A black beret was perched on his head and, as he came closer, Renzo could see he also wore a sheepskin cloak over a worn-out coat, which in turn covered a purple shirt. His baggy corduroy pants extended long enough to almost hide a pair of mud-covered boots. A pipe hung from the corner of his mouth, and large puffs of smoke trailed behind him.

As the man approached Renzo, Nino, and Captain Benelli, he stared at them with a look of disbelief in his eyes. He removed the pipe from his mouth, revealing a few yellow teeth amid mostly bare gums, and blew a waft of nauseating smoke in their direction. Eyeing the captain, he defiantly let out a jet of spit that landed on the dusty road, just missing the captain's feet. Then, with a brisk pull on the reins and a guttural grunt, he steered the donkey to his left and continued on his way.

The captain, obviously incensed by the shepherd's offensive gesture, stood erect and, in bad French, yelled, *"Fermez vous, fermez vous!"* mistakenly telling the peasant "shut" instead of "stop." Renzo was fairly fluent in French, having studied it for three years, but he stood in silence, choosing not to correct the captain. Benelli's face turned crimson, his hands were visibly trembling. The shepherd surveyed the long convoy of trucks and the number of cannons now taking up a large part of the surrounding area. He shook his head, shrugged, and continued on.

"Stop, you savage beast, or I'll have you shot!" he ordered, fuming with rage. The man ignored him. "Crespi, tell him what I said."

Renzo translated the captain's words exactly.

The shepherd shouted a command, and the donkey stopped along with the dogs and his flock. The old man slowly slid off his braying donkey and, showing no signs of fear, walked back, reins in hand, to stand face-to-face with the captain.

"Search this peasant," Captain Benelli ordered. Nino jumped to the task. Apparently the captain was looking for some sort of weapon, believing the shepherd might have been part of the underground sent out to spy on them.

The old man stood proudly erect, staring fiercely at Nino as he searched his clothing. He redirected his intense gaze toward Captain Benelli as Nino looked into the saddlebag hanging across the donkey's back. His sheepskin bag, however, contained only a loaf of hard, homemade bread, a piece of fresh cheese, a few chestnuts, and a clay flask full of wine. There was no pistol in his satchel, no carbines under his cloak, and no hand grenades in his pockets. The swelling in one of his coat pockets was only a leather pouch, half-full of foul-smelling homegrown tobacco.

Renzo watched as Nino followed the captain's orders and came to a conclusion: the captain's failure to dominate or frighten the aloof peasant had infuriated him immensely. Renzo sensed the seeds of paranoia beginning to sprout from Captain Benelli's bruised ego. The captain rolled down his sleeves and buttoned his shirt, his face still purple with indignation.

The shepherd, following the captain's every move with curiosity, pulled his beret over his brow until it almost covered his eyes, removed the pipe from his mouth, murmured a curse in his Corsican patois, and spat on the ground once again. "Who are you anyway? And what are you doing here?" the peasant asked in a coarse, loud voice.

Renzo translated, realizing his skills would be needed frequently for the captain. As if trying to reestablish his identity, the captain reached inside the ambulance and took out a riding whip he always carried with him. He pointed with the whip to the silver stars on his shirt collar and, through Renzo, he and the shepherd had a brief conversation.

"I'll tell you who I am," Captain Benelli replied to the crusty old man. "I am the captain of these troops and am now the sole authority in this district." He paused to clear his throat and then, with renewed vigor, he continued. "Is there a mayor in this town?"

"Of course," said the shepherd.

"Where can I find him?"

"Why do you need to know?"

"That's not your concern. Keep in mind, I am in charge here now. Don't force me to use my authority. I've been lenient toward you so far."

The shepherd stared at the captain, hesitating but then relenting. "He lives only a short distance away on this road, in the house around the bend facing the cliff."

The captain dismissed the shepherd with a wave of the back of his hand, indicating the encounter was over. He then turned to Nino, saying, "Come on, then. Let's pay him a visit."

The peasant gave one final glare toward the captain and walked away, leading his donkey and commanding the dogs to gather the sheep and continue their journey.

To Renzo's amazement, the captain suddenly regained the composure of a conqueror. His face brightened and his eyes sparkled with renewed confidence. With more hand motions than words, he then asked his orderly to dust off his knee-high boots and to brush the dust from his uniform. He obviously wanted to establish a respectable image, as he hoped to impress the mayor. The captain thrived on praise and always tried to solicit it from his superiors, his peers, or his subordinates. "Join us, Renzo," Benelli said. "You can make sure there are no misunderstandings between me and the mayor."

Monocled, with riding whip in hand, the captain departed, accompanied by Renzo and Nino. An hour later, they returned. A wide, genuine grin covered the captain's face.

"We have a home! We have a home!" he shouted repeatedly to everyone within hearing distance. With unrestrained enthusiasm, he waved a set of house keys above his head. The troops stopped their activities and circled the captain. "I met the mayor, and he obviously was expecting me," he recounted, filled with childlike joy. "He was very polite and respectful. He's a bit skinny and wears thick spectacles. Not a very imposing man. He stuttered when he spoke to me, obviously impressed by my rank. We politely exchanged some diplomatic formalities but most important, I made it a point to emphasize that because the island is under military rule and the village is under my rule, it would be advisable for him to fully cooperate with me. I asked whether there were any accommodations in the village for us. It turns out that the big house next door to the mayor is empty and has been for some time—the owners moved to America. The mayor gave me the keys. And here they are!" exclaimed the jubilant captain, again circling the keys over his head.

****

The house was not a palace, but it certainly was preferable to sleeping in tents. An ancient two-story stone structure with ten rooms on each floor, it appeared as if it was once a roadside hotel. A high wall, made from granite quarried nearby, surrounded it, keeping it out of view from the road. Its courtyard was long and wide. A couple of abandoned bocce courts lay alongside the carriage house. Four evergreen trees, with cement and stone rings at their base to serve as benches, lined the west wall. An immense chestnut tree in the center of the yard dominated the entire property. A large, uncultivated garden, still filled with withered plants and dead rose bushes, completed the grounds.

Captain Benelli ordered some of the soldiers to install the cannons in strategic positions along the edge of the cliff. Renzo and Nino worked with the remaining troops to make the house livable. Except for a few chairs and a couple of desks, there was no furniture in the house. The truckload of hay that General Headquarters had sent was divided among the men for their sleeping needs. They each folded one of their blankets and sewed it along three edges, making a sack of it. Then they filled it with hay to serve as a straw bed.

The captain had requisitioned a room for himself. The soldiers could hear him all through the night, moaning and cursing at his orderly—in an effort to please the captain, Nino had overstuffed the captain's sack, which made it too round and caused him to roll off it and onto the cold, cement-tiled floor.

$$****$$

There wasn't any need for reveille the following morning. As soon as the day broke, the captain was shouting all sorts of profanities aimed at his orderly, followed by a familiar cry, "Oh, my aching back!"

It was such an urgent cry that Renzo had to postpone the distribution of the quinine pills that morning. Captain Benelli's massage took priority. The captain grumbled at length, loudly and with disgust.

"I deserve better accommodations than this wretched house. After all, I am now the highest authority in the village. Am I not the most decorated commander of the most elite company in the regiment?"

Renzo silently continued the massage, knowing the captain just needed to blow off some steam.

"Whoever heard of an officer of my caliber being forced to sleep on the floor? And a Corsican floor to boot! This can't be!" Come what may, he swore that he was going to get the best accommodations the village had to offer. The dignity of his rank had to be protected, along with the fragility of his back.

****

After breakfast, still mumbling and furious and with horsewhip in hand, Captain Benelli hastened to the mayor's house for the second time, with Renzo and Nino at his side. He minced no words with the mayor. "Who owns the best home in this town?" he asked through Renzo.

"M-m-monsieur Santi, of c-course!" stuttered the puzzled mayor.

"How do I get there?"

The mayor pointed. "T-turn right at the c-corner and climb to the end. It's the l-lone house at the top of the hill."

Hurriedly, they proceeded in that direction with the realization that by now, their presence in the village was surely known. Renzo had become more aware of the citizens' adverse reaction. As they went up the hill, he could see old women peering out of slightly opened window shutters, followed by their slamming them shut as the three passed. The captain, however, was completely oblivious to all of that. He rehearsed how to approach this Monsieur Santi, whoever he was, and what to say to him. Should he seize a whole section of the house or just ask for Monsieur Santi's cooperation in giving him a room at his disposal? He found fault with each option—one was too pretentious and abrasive; the other, too meek and too demeaning for a man of his stature.

When they reached the side entrance, Captain Benelli knocked at the door with quick strokes of the thick end of his riding whip. Although he was out of breath, he obviously was ready to roar. But once the door opened, he froze up, speechless. A distinguished, delicate-looking, gray-haired lady stood in front of them. Probably in her sixties, she leaned on a highly polished black wooden cane with a silver dog head as its handle. She peered at the men over a pair of silver-framed spectacles. "It is indeed a pleasure that you call on us, Monsieur Capitaine," she said, obviously recognizing his rank. "To what do I owe the honor of your visit?"

Clearly, the finesse, grace, and courtesy with which he had been welcomed had disarmed the captain. Almost stuttering, he simply managed to say, "May I speak to Monsieur Santi?"

"He's not at home at the moment," she said in a soft, gentle voice. "I am Madame Santi. Is there anything I can do for you, Monsieur Capitaine?"

Captain Benelli hesitated but then explained the unfortunate situation he was in and that, because of the precarious state of his health, he would be eternally grateful if he could be accepted as a guest in their lovely home. The petulance he had displayed during the conversation he'd had with himself on the way up had turned into a plea. Suddenly, he had become humble, a side of him Renzo had never seen. "All I need is a room with a comfortable bed in it. My government will remunerate you handsomely," he said. "But, of course, if you can't make such a decision, I will return later on and speak to Monsieur Santi."

"Oh, no," Madame Santi insisted firmly. "There's no need for that. We want no compensation, and I assure you, Monsieur Santi and I will be happy to have an honored guest such as you in our home. We do indeed have an extra bedroom in the house and certainly, you are welcome to it. We will make it ready for you by evening," she said, with the grace of a queen. Without hesitation, she then gave him the key to a guest room that had an entrance from the veranda, facing the courtyard, where he would have complete privacy, assuring him that he would never be disturbed.

****

Pleased at the way things had worked out, the men returned to the big house, where a motorcycle messenger from headquarters was waiting for the captain. The messenger greeted Benelli and delivered two messages, which Benelli later posted at the main entrance of the house. The first read:

For the grace of God and the will of the nation, Vittorio Emanuele, king of Italy and emperor of Ethiopia: On this day—November 11, 1942—declares officially that the occupation of Corsica has been completed successfully. My best wishes to the generals in charge and all officers and soldiers who have brought their task to an end with honor, valor, and distinction.

Vittorio Emanuele

The second message was from the general commander of the division. It was a specific four-point guideline of behavior:

I—The dignity of a proud soldier should always be maintained.
II—No permit or furlough will be issued to anyone.
III—Shoulder weapons should always be carried on a state of alert.
IV—Under severe penalty of imprisonment adequate to the indiscretion committed, any association with the civilian population is absolutely prohibited.

These severe restricting orders, although somber and somewhat foreboding, failed to dampen the captain's rejuvenated spirit. With renewed confidence, he made up a schedule so that each of the soldiers, in turn, would share the task of escorting him to his room. The privilege of being the first fell on Renzo. And so, when night descended, they climbed the hill to the Santis' house.

Captain Benelli entered through his private door. Renzo waited outside in silence, not only to absorb the stillness of the night but also to wonder whether his demanding and overbearing captain was finally pleased with his newly found accommodations. The answer came shortly. As he stood on the veranda, Renzo noticed that the captain had blown out the kerosene lamp in his room. And then, soon after, he was absolutely convinced that Captain Francesco Maria Giancarlo Benelli was happy. Very happy, indeed! He heard him sneeze. Twice.

3   *Christmas*

November had gone by quietly, as had most of December. In that time, the men in the company had accomplished much. The rooms in the big house were whitewashed, the windowpanes cleaned, and the floors scrubbed and disinfected. An outdoor kitchen was built against the south wall. Makeshift showers and other items for personal needs were improvised on the east wall, away from the mayor's house.

Contrary to Captain Benelli's high opinion of himself and his men, they were not the elite company of the regiment. They were neither better nor worse than any other company, yet they were an interesting group of men. They comprised a cross section of Italian youths from almost every region and district of Italy—a mixture of young men with various backgrounds ranging from college students to journeymen farmers with little or no formal education.

Although they were all members of one single group, trained for the same military missions, they shared very few general characteristics. Other than the uniform they wore, there were few common bonds. They all had their own opinions, their own ideals, their own ambitions, and their own dreams.

There were the zealots, and there were the passives. There were those who volunteered for everything, eager to please and to win the approval—and maybe some favors—from the captain, and there were those who would find all sorts of excuses to shirk the responsibility of their assigned duties. Yet in spite of these differences, they all managed to get along without incident. They knew, since first coming together nearly a year earlier in Livorno, that they had to trust their lives to each other.

****

Captain Benelli ordered the carriage house be used as the station for the guards on duty for the twenty-four-hour watch period. There had been no imminent threats to their safety since their arrival, but an undercurrent of danger always lurked. The Corsican underground was active, though incognito, throughout the island. There were rumors from other parts of Corsica of arrests of people plotting against the Italian army. No official reports were issued, but the possibility of an attack remained real.

Renzo set up his infirmary on the ground floor, sandwiched between the captain's office and what was to become the office of the sergeant in charge of clerical work. The infirmary was nothing more than an oversized first-aid station, solely intended to assist the company in case of minor ailments or injuries. For more serious cases, it was Renzo's job to transport the soldiers to any of eight field hospitals in Corsica. So far, there had only been a few cuts and bruises resulting from the work being done on the house—not everyone was adept at using tools—which Renzo's training prepared him to treat.

In order to give the command post a distinct identity, the men decided to name the building. Disregarding Il Duce's ordinance that no foreign word contaminate the Italian language, the soldiers, in a mock ceremony, dubbed it "La Grande Maison"—French for "The Big House"—while on the lintel above the front door, they placed a sign inscribed in Italian, a quote from Dante's *Divine Comedy*: "Lasciate ogni speranza, voi ch'entrate"—"Abandon hope, all ye who enter here."

****

Each morning began the same, with Renzo mindlessly drawing an X through the previous day's date on the calendar that hung on the wall next to his bunk. He looked at the new date and sighed.

Friday
December 25, 1942
Christmas Day

Christmas, Renzo thought, *and I'm sitting in this stupid place.*

Most of the company had gone to a field mass at the Citadel, the seat of headquarters. Only the guards on duty and a few other men, including Renzo, remained at La Grande Maison to maintain a minimal staff. The one change in town that Renzo noticed was the festive sound of church bells. Captain Benelli had previously forbidden the priest from ringing the bells, fearing that it could be a secret signal calling for insurrection. But the ban had been lifted for Christmas Day, and the bells were clanging, joyfully calling the villagers to church.

Renzo went outdoors and stood by the gate, watching a stream of mostly elderly women come from the side streets and walk toward the church. He had seen these women previously, going about the village, always dressed in black. As was their custom, they never left their homes without wearing their *mantilla*—a large kerchief, usually black, somberly wrapped around their shoulders or tied under their chins as a head cover. But today was different. For Christmas, the women wore long, colorful dresses that reached the ground. Neatly dressed, noisy children followed them—boys with slickly combed hair and girls whose hair was tied up with pretty bows.

Renzo remained by the gate until long after the last person had entered the church and the road had become completely deserted and silent. He felt nostalgic for his family and friends. He was alone in a foreign land, in an unfamiliar and potentially hostile environment, surrounded by people he didn't know, people who wished he wasn't there. He became mindful of the uncertainty of his future.

Although lost in thought, Renzo was suddenly aware of the rhythmic click of high-heeled shoes on the cobblestone road to his left. A young woman dressed in a stylish, light-blue tailored suit, with pale blue shoes and a white silk scarf loosely wrapped around her slim neck passed him without a look or a casual glance, as if he weren't even there. She was beautiful, with thick black hair visible beneath a small, white veil that barely covered the top of her head. Renzo felt an instant attraction. Without thinking of any potential consequences of his actions, Renzo followed her to church at a discreet distance, leaving his post without notifying anyone.

****

Renzo entered the church, L'église Saint-Rocco, and quickly scanned his surroundings while looking for the girl. The doors were carved black wood, as were all the statues and the pulpit. The walls were covered with brocade, and multicolored velvet drapes framed the windows. Dominating the center altar was a huge brown wooden statue of Christ, at whose feet was the manger where the newborn Jesus slept. On the side altar, a statue of Saint Rocco, patron saint of the shepherds, was prominently placed, surrounded by freshly cut wildflowers. The pungent smell of incense and lighted candles permeated the church.

Renzo's eyes continued to roam. Although the Mass had already started, it didn't surprise him that his presence had not gone unnoticed and had caused a stir among the parishioners. One woman saw him and nudged the woman next to her. They turned to look at him, and the nudging and turning continued from pew to pew. Some people scowled, some shook their heads, but they looked away quickly. Ignoring them, he finally found where the girl in the pale blue suit was seated.

She was the only one who had not turned her head to look at him. Seated at the far right in the third pew, she remained kneeled in prayer, looking toward the altar. She didn't seem to be anything like the other Corsican women. She appeared to be as much out of place as he was.

Who is she? Where is she from? It was obvious she wasn't with any of the other congregants. She had come alone and sat apart from the others. Renzo tried to get a better sense of her appearance but since she was facing the wrong way, his view of her from the street had been better. With her hands raised in front of her face, palm to palm, he did, however, have a good view of her left hand. There was no wedding ring.

Suddenly, Renzo realized he wasn't in full uniform. He had broken all the rules, leaving his post bareheaded and without his sidearm. He knew he should return to La Grande Maison but didn't want to draw any more attention to himself by leaving while Mass was still in progress. He waited in the back until it was over and watched as the church quickly emptied. He decided to follow the girl and attempt to strike up a conversation—she would most likely go back the way she came, in the direction of La Grande Maison.

Just as Renzo was leaving the church, he felt an urgent, repeated tug on his arm. It was the altar boy, who politely told him that the priest wanted to see him. That invitation, flattering as it was, couldn't have come at a worse time. It forced Renzo to make a quick decision. Should he snub the priest's invitation and follow the girl in the pale blue suit or go to the priest and give up the opportunity to meet the beautiful young woman? He didn't have time to think. He knew this opportunity might never come again. But by the time he turned his eyes away from the altar boy and stretched his neck through the doorway for another look, she had already disappeared. He looked at the backs of the parishioners as they walked away from the church, but he couldn't see her anywhere. *Damn!*

****

Turning back to the altar boy, Renzo nodded. He was taken to the rectory, where he met the priest, a jovial, rotund old man, almost seventy, with sparse white hair, lively eyes, and a quick smile that displayed a set of yellowish, uneven teeth.

"*Bon Noël, mon ami.* May Jesus Christ be praised," the priest said, bending slightly at the waist, hands together as if in prayer. "I am Padre Silvestri, pastor and servant of Saint Rocco's Church." He extended his arms and took Renzo's hand into both of his, pumping it vigorously.

"Bon Noël to you, Padre. I am Renzo Crespi. As you can see, I am a soldier," he said gesturing to his uniform. He tried to show respect to the priest but inwardly was unhappy that his quest for the girl had been interrupted. He felt trapped and disappointed.

"You seem to be absent, mon ami. Is something troubling you? Is it because you are away from home on Christmas Day?" Padre Silvestri asked in a benevolent and comforting tone, making Renzo blush with guilt—he was about to lie.

"Oh, no, Father, thank you," he hurriedly apologized. "It's just that I have lost touch with civilian life. I have forgotten my manners. Please forgive me."

The priest said nothing. He just smiled and nodded.

"Besides," Renzo continued, "I am still in awe of the beauty of your church. I am so impressed!"

"Yes, it is beautiful. It's one of the oldest churches in Corsica. Come with me; I'll show you the grounds." The padre beamed with pride and, bowing lightly, indicated with arms outstretched that Renzo should head for the back door.

As they went around the church's courtyard, Renzo noticed that Padre Silvestri was somewhat unsteady on his legs. Looking at him more closely, he suspected that the padre's hands shook almost constantly, as he saw that various stains of dried-up food of different sizes and colors had been spilled all along his worn-out, faded tunic. His mind, however, was lucid and his speech crisp and sure. He showed Renzo his garden that overlooked the lush green valley, while all along discussing the village and its inhabitants. It was from him that Renzo got a clearer picture of the Corsican mind and nature: who, why, and what they are. The priest began with the men.

"You will find the Corsicans to be grave and reserved private men, occasionally melancholy and always brooding. They are faithful to their traditions and to their friends. They are prone to take offense easily and can be quite vindictive. They are born fighters and will remain fighters to their last breath. They curse God easily, and just as easily, they ask His forgiveness. Although most of the peasants are illiterate, they could recite from memory complete stanzas from the great poets, including whole passages from Dante's *Divine Comedy*. They nourish a morbid and everlasting affection for their dead, who cast a gloomy mantle on their lives." He smiled as he concluded, "They love their land and they are fiercely attached to it, but they don't want to work it."

As he spoke, Padre Silvestri would stop his dissertation and slow down his pace to raise his tunic off the ground so it wouldn't drag over the little aromatic plants. He continued, but in fewer words, giving his opinion of the Corsican women. "The women occupy a position of inferiority. Their life is simple and uncomplicated. I can describe it in three words—work, sacrifice, and submission.

Their youth is brief, and they age prematurely. But as passive and submissive as they are, they can easily become furies, if or when there is a question of vendetta or revenge."

Renzo found Padre Silvestri's explanation of his people an unexpected yet informative revelation. He would have liked to stay and hear more, but it was time to leave. Before going, Renzo had one question. "Why do the people have such an open hatred for us? Most of your parishioners looked at me with obvious contempt."

Once again the priest held Renzo's hand in both of his. Looking straight into Renzo's eyes, he said in a voice that begged for understanding, "Don't be so harsh in judging our people. It's more fear than hatred. You see, dear Renzo, you have your restrictions; we have ours. Any one of us caught associating with the soldiers will eventually be prosecuted for being a collaborator. Not by a court of justice, mind you, but by the Maquisards, the underground units who are growing on the island every day. You don't see them. You don't know where they are or who they are, but they are there, somewhere, watching."

For Renzo, those last words were a ringing admonition that he should never neglect or forget that advice. Renzo had already heard about the Maquisards, named for the maquis, the dense, spiny scrubland that gave refuge to bandits and fugitives over the centuries. With cells throughout France, they relied on guerrilla tactics to harass the occupation troops. The Maquisards also aided the escape of downed Allied airmen, Jews, and others pursued by the Vichy and German authorities. Maquisards usually relied on some degree of sympathy or cooperation from the local populace but often instilled fear into citizens whose behavior was suspect.

Once Renzo began to walk on the deserted road toward La Grande Maison, everything Padre Silvestri had told him vanished from his mind. The clicking sound of high-heeled shoes on the cobblestone road still echoed in his ears. Despite the priest's comments, Renzo remained determined to learn who she was, where she came from, and how he could find her.

4 *Searching*

enzo didn't tell anyone about his experience at St. Rocco's and intended to keep it that way for two reasons. First, it simply wasn't anybody else's business; second—and most important—he didn't want anyone to know that he had dared to leave his post without permission.

New Year's Day didn't come quickly enough for him. With much anticipation, he was dressed and ready to go at the crack of dawn. Like a racehorse at the starting gate about to sprint, he stood impatiently waiting for the clicking sound of high heels on the cobblestone road so that he could start his trek to church. Ten minutes. Fifteen minutes. Could he have missed her? He had longed the entire week for this day, and he could no longer wait. Although the sun had barely pierced through the mild winter-morning fog, he raced to St. Rocco's, where he hoped to once again see the mysterious young woman who had been in his thoughts since Christmas Day. Renzo's eyes scanned every congregant, methodically looking at every pew. Not seeing her, he waited until the Mass was over and watched as all the parishioners departed. But she wasn't one of them.

He had planned all week what he would say to her when they finally met on New Year's Day, but those plans came to naught. From then on, for the entire month, he waited at the gate every Sunday, hoping to see her pass La Grande Maison, and each Sunday his heart sank a little deeper. When he didn't see her pass, he retreated into La Grande Maison without going to St. Rocco's. He justified her absence by assuming she was just a Christmas visitor in the village and had returned to her home soon after the holiday, wherever that was. But he quickly dismissed that reason. His intuition insisted she was from the village.

Renzo spent many sleepless nights trying to understand why he had been so unexplainably attracted to a complete stranger who, according to headquarters, he was supposed to consider an enemy. He still felt that he needed to find her and should start looking for her.

His behavior was noticeably changing. Contrary to his natural instinct to help anyone in need of assistance, he was now inattentive and apathetic. One morning he was checking the inventory of his supplies in the infirmary when Nino walked in, waving an envelope.

"Renzo, I received mail. Would you read it for me?"

Startled at the intrusion, Renzo dropped some packages of gauze. He turned and screamed at Nino, "Can't you see I'm in the middle of something? Is your stupid letter more important than my duties?"

Nino was stunned. He opened his eyes wide, and his jaw went slack. Backing out of the infirmary and reaching for the door, he could only say, "I'm sorry to have bothered you."

Everyone at La Grande Maison noticed the abrupt change in Renzo's conduct, to the point that his fellow soldiers were saying he had become uncaring and unapproachable—or perhaps ill.

To increase his chances of finding the girl, he volunteered to be included on the roster of active police patrol, even though he was exempt from those duties because of his other responsibilities. He assumed his odds would be increased if he were on patrol.

And so he began a daily, intense quest. He canvassed every little street and alleyway and made every possible effort to locate her. Over the next few months, whenever he had some free time, he visited every house, every hut, and every hovel in the village, as well as every hamlet in the company's jurisdiction. Relentlessly, he kept on with his door-to-door inquisition, asking questions. "How many people live here? Who are they? Did you have any guests at Christmas?" His efforts yielded nothing, other than suspicious stares and halting responses from the inhabitants, indicating their deep mistrust of their occupiers and everyone who represented them.

Gradually, he became acutely aware that the thin line that separates a mild case of sadness from madness was beginning to erode. He knew his obsession was pointless, and there were times when he believed he already was on the brink of losing his mind. Nevertheless, he continued to pretend to be happy at La Grande Maison. But as the days went by, it became obvious to everyone that something was wrong with him. He wasn't eating, wasn't able to sleep, and was always fatigued.

Captain Benelli came down to the infirmary one morning and approached Renzo, who was mopping the floor.

"Renzo, you've seemed a bit detached lately. Is something wrong?"

Renzo stopped and leaned on the mop. He had no explanation, but thinking quickly, he looked the captain squarely in his eyes and lied. "I know, Captain. My mind has been preoccupied. I assume you know about the exam that will be held in Italy in May for all university students in the army. I've been studying every spare moment I have. Also, depending on the needs of the army when the time comes, I'm afraid I may be denied a furlough to be able to take the test."

"Give the books a rest for a while," the captain said in encouragement. "You will get your furlough. And you will get through the exams just fine. The board of examiners is lenient to servicemen. Besides," he continued, with a patronizing wink, "I have strong connections, and I can pull a few strings for you." He patted Renzo on his shoulders and asked with obvious pride, "How about that?"

Renzo meekly agreed and thanked the captain for his unsolicited and kind cooperation. But he knew better. He knew the truth.

5   *Confession to a Friend*

Renzo's closest friend in the company was Alvaro Tonelli, a lanky, sophisticated man with blond hair and bright, laughing blue eyes. He was from the Emilia region, and his father owned one of the most prolific silkworm farms and the largest mulberry orchard in northern Italy. The senior Tonelli belonged to the new breed of Fascist aristocracy and had been knighted *"cavaliere"* by Benito Mussolini for his efforts and contribution to the Italian silk industry.

Alvaro Tonelli had gone to the University of Reggio Emilia to pursue a degree in agriculture, which would prepare him to take over his father's business. He was the motorcycle dispatcher for the company and had been assigned to help Renzo in the infirmary and if he needed assistance with the ambulance. He often boasted about his romantic conquests and that women found him attractive—they couldn't help themselves. According to Tonelli, he'd noticed since boyhood that his popularity with girls steadily increased, making him the life of each party he attended. He was convinced that he had become both a menace and a blessing to the female sex, to the point that it had become necessary for him to keep a list of his innumerable sexual conquests.

Never out of words, Tonelli could sweet-talk his way into or out of anything. Yet, although he occasionally behaved like an outrageous snob and a spoiled rich playboy, Renzo had grown to like him. He had a certain charisma that made him pleasant and acceptable.

Because Tonelli's way of thinking was diametrically opposed to

Renzo's conservative nature, Renzo initially was standoffish toward him. But since they both slept in the infirmary and were forced to spend a large amount of time together, they slowly accepted each other and had become friends.

Tonelli was also a talented musician, having a mastery of the guitar. Renzo admired the instrument every time Alvaro played it. It had two separate, highly polished mahogany fingerboards. One was at the center, with six strings like any conventional guitar, and the other, with four bass strings, was just above it. Both rosewood fingerboards were elaborately decorated with many inlaid mother-of-pearl fleur-de-lis designs.

Although Tonelli always appeared totally self-absorbed, he noticed Renzo's erratic behavior. He didn't say anything until one evening, when every off-duty soldier was outdoors, drinking wine and singing as the cook played his accordion. Renzo, who was much too deeply absorbed in his own thoughts to join in, had decided to remain inside the infirmary. Tonelli was with him, a cigarette hanging from his lips as he practiced an intricate piece of classical music on his guitar. Renzo was lying on his cot, vacantly staring at the ceiling.

Tonelli stopped playing, rose from his wooden stool, and slowly and carefully leaned his guitar straight up against the whitewashed wall. Renzo's eyes were still half-closed, but he observed Alvaro pick up his stool and place it on the tiled floor in line with Renzo's head. Alvaro sat down with his legs apart, his hands folded, and his arms hanging loose between his knees. An impish smile crossed his face as he leaned forward and asked, "What's the matter, my friend?"

"What makes you think there's anything the matter?"

"I haven't seen you crack a smile for quite a while. I haven't heard you speak a word for a long time. There has to be something troubling you."

"Well, there isn't," Renzo snapped.

"See? There you are! I've only asked you a friendly question, and you're already angry at me!" He paused briefly to consider. "*Are* you angry at me?"

"No. I'm not."

"Are you feeling all right?"

"I'm fine, I assure you."

"Have you received bad news from home?"

"No."

"What is it, then? I'm concerned about you. I don't know what to make of it. Look at yourself. You look terrible. What is it?"

Renzo was getting annoyed by the interrogation. He was touched to know that there was someone who really cared for him, but stubbornly, he remained silent for a while longer. Finally, he spoke. "It's those stupid books!" Renzo said. "I have exams coming soon, but no matter how much I study, nothing sticks in my head." The excuse had worked with Captain Benelli, but it didn't work for the cagey Tonelli.

"Studying?" Tonelli mocked. "Now I know you're lying! You haven't touched your books in a long time. Look at them!" He picked up one of the books from Renzo's shelf. "They're full of dust!" he blurted out, loudly blowing the dust off its cover. "Come on now, Renzo. I'm your friend. Tell me what's wrong," Tonelli pleaded. "Maybe I can help."

Tonelli's barrage of questions and sincere concern had not only weakened Renzo's resistance but also made him realize he did need help. The two men had previously revealed private thoughts to each other, particularly about their personal lives, politics, and the war, and in doing so had developed enough trust for one another to become good friends. Counting on Tonelli's discretion and secrecy, Renzo quietly confided in him about the girl, as he would have to an older brother.

Tonelli listened attentively, nodding frequently. Renzo, now exhausted, had disclosed everything, all the while watching Tonelli's facial expressions, which ranged from simple curiosity to acute interest. "Very romantic!" Tonelli commented. "But love? It sounds like a schoolboy crush. You haven't even spoken with her."

That sort of comment didn't surprise Renzo at all. He knew that Tonelli considered love just a sloppy sentimentality, having no substance and timidly expressed only by pimpled teenagers.

"Oh, yes, it's love. I assure you," Renzo said, exposing his naiveté with every word. "I felt something inside when I saw her that I can't explain. She is breathtakingly beautiful and graceful."

"Beautiful, you say." Tonelli now appeared interested.

"She's an angel," Renzo answered.

"Hold it now, Renzo. You're running away from me," Tonelli said, trying to control Renzo's enthusiasm.

"Yes," Renzo said. "I believe she is my ideal woman. We would be perfect for each other. It's fate, you know!"

A puzzled look now covered Tonelli's face. "Come on now, Renzo. Wake up!" He snapped his fingers as if he wanted to bring Renzo out of a hypnotic state. "No woman is an angel. Women are not at all like angels. Women are more like horses!"

Renzo gave Tonelli a quizzical look and moved to sit on the side of the bed, anticipating an explanation. "I beg your pardon?"

"Yes, yes," Tonelli continued. "Let me explain. You see, there are three breeds of horses, as there are three types of women. There is the show horse, the one who wins the blue ribbon at the fair, which is like the fancy lady you escort to the opera for everyone to see and admire. Then there is the thoroughbred, the horse that wins first prize at the racetrack, which is like the lady who takes first place at a beauty contest. And finally, there is the workhorse. That's the horse that for a bale of hay will work all day for you, much the same as the domestic woman who, for the pleasure of your company, would submit to anything. Now, of course, if by luck you could find a woman possessing all those qualities, it would be like having found a horse who could win a blue ribbon at the fair, win a race, and pull a plow, if necessary."

"That's an absurd, preposterous analogy!" Renzo exploded. "This kind of talk is repugnant to me!"

"I was only joking—can't you tell?" Tonelli said, seeming somewhat apologetic.

"I'm not laughing. Can't *you* tell?" Renzo's reaction appeared to surprise Tonelli, but Renzo continued. "Don't be so facetious, Tonelli. Stop this foolishness and make some sense. Be serious for once, will you?"

"I was only trying to bring a smile to your face."

"Well, I'm not amused!"

Unruffled, Tonelli went on. "All right. You want me to be serious? Fine. But I tell you, you're not going to like it," he admonished.

Slowly, he rose from his stool and paced the floor as if he were preparing to lecture Renzo. "My first suggestion is that you give up this futile chase."

"What?" Renzo said, surprised at Tonelli's snappy decision.

"Yes," Tonelli said, "for two reasons. First, because I'm sure that you're not going to find her here. A girl like the one you've described doesn't belong in a backward, unsophisticated, miserable village like this. Obviously, she's a city girl. I'm sure she must be from Corte or Bastia or Ajaccio. You should be looking there." He paused again briefly to catch his breath and then continued. "And reason number two, what would your chances be, once you do find her, that she would fall for you or even give you a second look? Are you forgetting that we are enemies, and we are not allowed to associate with them or they with us? They would just as soon spit in your face or, if given a chance, throw piss on you, as they did in Bastia."

Tonelli took a deep breath, and Renzo could see he had become livid with anger. His face was flushed, and his hands were trembling. That unfortunate episode was still fresh in his mind and had triggered his wrath. "You just told me about the unwelcoming stares you received from the parishioners on Christmas Day and the reaction of the villagers during your search. Don't forget—none of them wants us here, including your angel."

The logic of Tonelli's reasoning was no longer nonsense to Renzo. That explosive lecture had shown him a side of Tonelli that he hadn't expected to see. Until then, Renzo had the impression that Alvaro was strictly a spoiled, senseless playboy, bent only on physical pleasure and nothing else. But there also was a serious side to him. His observations had made Renzo see that beneath a veneer of brashness, arrogance, and superficiality, there existed a sensible human being—a man who had to be appreciated for his openness, his common sense, the keen awareness of life as it actually was, and most of all, his attempt to put Renzo in touch with the reality of the situation. Yet, although Tonelli had apparently helped Renzo think more logically about the girl, they were no nearer to a solution.

Tonelli reached for his guitar. "I'm going to play one of your favorite songs," he said, drumming his fingers on his guitar in a slow, deliberate rhythm.

"Tosti?" Renzo asked, immensely pleased.

"Yes. I promise it will be a safety valve for you. It will lessen your pain and restore your morale."

As Tonelli's fingers plucked the strings, the sweet sound of that melodic, romantic song had the opposite effect—it filled Renzo's heart with determination. When the song ended he was still unconvinced that he should abandon his search. He preferred to take his chances and face his destiny on his own terms.

The night ended as it had begun. Tonelli was still fingering his guitar, and Renzo was still lying on his cot with his eyes fixed on the ceiling, thinking about the lady in the pale-blue tailored suit who was still beckoning him.

6   *A Lucky Break*

Renzo spent February and March still haunted by the mysterious woman, although time managed to lessen his melancholy over not finding her, and his enthusiasm for normal activities had returned. He gave up his search, along with the patrol duties, but remained certain that someday he would find her. He accepted the reality of the situation and gradually regained a more constructive sense of normalcy.

Tonelli contributed greatly to Renzo's improved mood. His encouragement and soothing music helped to lower Renzo's anxieties and raise his morale and self-esteem.

Captain Benelli, believing Renzo was tormented by his studies, also cooperated. He was well aware of Renzo's workload at the infirmary, so he kept the rigid schedule of backrubs to a minimum. However, one afternoon he came down from his private quarters and entered the infirmary looking somewhat ruffled and alarmed. He approached Renzo, who was treating one of the soldiers for a gash he'd received on his hand from an exposed nail in the carriage house. The captain's back was fine, but he had another matter of urgency. He asked about the soldier's injury and then placed his right hand on Renzo's shoulder; his expression was serious. "Renzo, I will be away for three days. I must go to Corte to meet General Magli." Magli recently had been named commander in chief of all the Italian forces in Corsica. "I will be presenting a status report of this sector."

"Yes, sir." Renzo was unsure why the captain needed to tell him this.

"Also, I need you to tend to Madame Santi. She has fallen and hurt herself."

"How badly is she hurt?"

"I don't know, but she is in terrible pain," he said. His eyes pleaded before he continued. "Please, Renzo, go. Do what you can. She will appreciate it, and I am sure that you won't regret it."

Renzo sensed the importance of the captain's request—it was the first time he had heard the word *please* come out of his mouth. Renzo quickly gathered his first-aid box and hurried on his way.

****

The Santis' house, a structure of pink granite nestled at the very top of the hill, dominated the entire village. It stood alone, like an eagle's nest surrounded by chestnut trees. A fence of prickly pears protected a well-kept garden. Hexagonal-shaped terra-cotta tiles led to the front door—a massive, hand-carved oak door with masterly crafted floral inlays. The door's central panel boasted a fist-sized bronze lion's head resting on a thick, round bronze plate. Renzo lifted the lion's head, knocked three times, and waited.

There wasn't much daylight left. Turning his back to the door, he watched as the sun slowly disappeared into the not-so-distant sea, leaving a reddish hue. The brilliant colors of sunset were yielding to the dusk. He had become so engrossed in watching the windswept evening clouds that he didn't hear the door behind him open.

"Would you please come in, *Monsieur le soldat*?" A lovely female voice shook him from his thoughts.

He turned around and thought his eyes were playing games with him. He closed them and opened them again but still couldn't believe what he was seeing. It wasn't a mirage! There, directly in front of him, stood the woman he had so desperately fallen in love with—the lady in the pale-blue tailored suit.

He wanted to speak but couldn't. He remained open-mouthed with a stupefied daze. But then he heard that voice again, soft and sensuous.

"Please come in. Grandmama is waiting for you."

Renzo couldn't believe his luck. His face flushed with excitement.

His long, frustrated search had ended. "Yes," he said, still amazed at finally finding her. "Of course."

"Please follow me," she said politely.

Renzo entered the hallway, and the young woman escorted him through the house and to the staircase that led to Madame Santi's bedroom. As she walked, she left the fragrance of jasmine drifting behind her, which Renzo inhaled deeply. He admired her shapely figure as she climbed the long, white marble staircase and watched her delicate hands with manicured nails glide smoothly over the polished wooden banister. Her polka-dot dress swayed and rustled in front of Renzo, gently and evenly, like a wheat field on a breezy summer day.

Neither spoke, and the silence was painful for Renzo—he had waited so long for this opportunity. Nervous as he was, he made an attempt at conversation. Pausing at the top of the staircase, he looked at her and asked, "Is Madame in bed?"

"No," she said curtly.

"Is she in pain?"

"Yes."

"What happened?"

"She'll tell you."

Renzo was all too aware of the war-created barrier that existed between the Italians and the Corsicans, yet he was taken aback by her succinct responses.

"Come in, young man. Come in," a gentle voice called as they reached the door to the bedroom. Madame Santi was sitting in a heavy, comfortable Bergère chair, her right leg resting on an antique English footstool. The ebony cane with the silver dog head rested on a massive bed that dominated the large room.

"Will you be all right, Grandmama?"

"Yes, dear. You can go." A thin smile offset the weariness that covered her face.

"*Bon soir*, Madame," Renzo said as he entered the room. "I am Renzo. Do you remember me?"

"Of course, I remember you," she said graciously. "You came up here with the captain on your arrival, correct?"

"Yes, I had that pleasure. I'm glad you didn't forget."

"How could I forget? One doesn't meet handsome soldiers every day, you know." Her voice was filled with warm affection.

"You are very kind, Madame. Thank you."

It was obvious that even in pain, Madame Santi had not lost her diplomatic charm, and although many women of her age would rant under such a stressful situation, she maintained an admirable quietness and serenity.

"How do you feel?" Renzo asked, pointing at her foot. "Does it hurt much?"

"I'm in pain, Renzo. Something must be broken," she said.

Although not a licensed practicing physician, Renzo was well along in his studies and had rudimentary skill in the art of bone setting. "Could you, please, tell me what happened?" he asked.

"I was outdoors, surveying the grounds to make plans for my rock garden, when I lost my balance. My foot hit a large rock."

Renzo began his examination. He started at the knee and moved on to the tibia and then continued sliding his hands down to her ankle and foot. Other than some swelling and a slight dislocation of the anklebone, he didn't find any fractures. He occasionally glanced up at Madame Santi to check her expression and ascertain if he was causing any pain, and he noticed how intently she followed every move he made to adjust her ankle. Upon completing his examination, he rubbed his hands together, pleased with the results.

"Is there going to be a rock garden this year?" the old woman asked.

"Yes, Madame," he said. "You will be able to get to it in no time. There are no fractures. It's only a light contusion, which won't last long."

She let out a sigh of relief, while making the sign of the cross.

"But to avoid any unwanted stress," Renzo explained, "it needs to be bandaged."

These last words sounded devious even to Renzo, for there was no real need of bandages. An overnight rest would have sufficed, but he wanted to see *her* again. And to justify his lie, he hid behind the adage, "All's fair in love and war."

It didn't take long to remove what was needed from his first-aid box. As he began to roll the gauze strip around Madame Santi's ankle he heard a burst of piano music from downstairs. He hadn't noticed the concert piano that he passed as he approached the stairs; his eyes had been occupied elsewhere.

Renzo quickly completed wrapping Madame Santi's ankle, and then, excusing himself, he rushed to the rail at the top of the stairs that overlooked the great room where the piano was. The young lady was sitting at the piano, her head proudly held back as her hands glided gracefully, in full control of the keys. Her heaving, lovely bosom sank and swelled with the same fury of the music. Renzo remained motionless for a few minutes and when he returned to repack his supplies, he saw Madame Santi's eyes beaming with joy.

"Chopin?" he asked.

"The Twelfth Etude."

"The Revolutionary?"

"Yes."

Madame Santi seemed pleased that he recognized the piece so quickly. "You like music, I see!"

"Very much, Madame."

"What do you think of her playing?"

"Marvelous, wonderful, and yet ..." He paused and looked into her waiting eyes.

"And yet?" she asked.

"And yet," he continued, "there seems to be some anxiety in her tempo."

"So you have also noticed it," she agreed. "I don't know why, but lately she's been doing that in almost everything she plays. She must be upset about something. I shall remind her of it ... if she lets me."

"She plays well, though," he reassured the doting grandmother.

"Yes, she does. She will go far someday. She has the talent and the determination to pursue a music career. The concert stage is her goal, and as soon as this war is over, she will return to the Paris Conservatory, where she has spent the last three years."

"Who is tutoring her until then?" Renzo asked.

"I am."

Madame Santi explained that she, too, had been a successful, renowned concert pianist in Europe in her younger days. But then, while on a concert tour in Corsica long ago, she met Monsieur

Santi, a young landowner and supporter of the arts, who offered her hospitality in his house during her stay.

Soon after, they fell in love and then, once she had satisfied her concert commitments, she stopped her travels, wed Monsieur Santi, and settled in Corsica to dedicate her life to him and their marriage, permanently. "And now," she concluded, rotating her hands in front of Renzo, so he could see her gnarled knuckles, "because of this cursed arthritis, I can no longer play. But even if only by osmosis, I can still perpetuate the joy of music in this house."

"You are a fortunate woman indeed. You know music, and you should consider yourself blessed."

"I know that I'm blessed," she said, nodding. "I also know and firmly believe that music, like the Bible, is a special message from God to mankind—one with words, the other with sound."

"Wonderful thought, Madame! I shall remember that in the future. But for now, get all the rest you can," Renzo urged. "I will return tomorrow to remove the bandages."

"Would you be able to join us for dinner tomorrow, Renzo? Monsieur Santi will be home then. He would love to meet you."

"And I would be happy to meet him, Madame."

"Stop at the kitchen for a while," she said. "My granddaughter will give you a little something to eat before you leave."

"Well, thank you."

"Good night, Renzo."

"Good night, Madame."

****

As Renzo descended the staircase, he began to think of a way to establish a one-on-one conversation with the young woman. She stood at the bottom of the stairs, feet solidly planted on the floor, looking assured and somewhat defiant. Her curt responses from their earlier conversation, along with her dazzling beauty and regal composure, intimidated Renzo.

With his eyes fixed on her, he miscounted the number of steps on the stairway. As he reached what he thought was the last step, his knees buckled under. He wound up sprawled on the shiny checkerboard-tile floor, with one leg twisted under his buttocks and the other against the wall in the opposite direction. His first-aid kit skidded noisily across the floor, coming to a stop under the concert piano. Renzo was mortified. No bones were broken, but his pride was shattered. His plans to impress her had crumbled. He struggled to his feet and apologized for his clumsiness. He was afraid she might laugh at him but hoped she would show some pity.

She did neither. Instead, she looked at him with a cool, expressionless glance. "Are you hurt?" she asked.

"No. I'm fine." Renzo brushed and straightened his uniform.

She turned and proceeded toward the kitchen, indicating that Renzo should follow her. A row of neatly arranged hand-hammered copper pots hung above a wood stove with four furnaces. The dinner table was neatly set. A plateful of roast lamb and a round, freshly baked loaf of bread was waiting for him. A bottle of sparkling red wine stood next to a brightly lit kerosene lamp.

"Please sit down," she said. "Grandmama wants me to serve." She suddenly stopped and corrected herself. "Grandmama wants me to give you some dinner."

Her voice and manner were calm and sure. Renzo sensed he was facing a proud Corsican woman who had trouble with the word "serve." Renzo became ill at ease. He wanted a way to open the avenue of communication, but in contrast to Madame Santi, who was friendly and approachable, this young woman appeared to be wrapped in a mantle of ice.

Renzo attempted to ingratiate himself. Without sounding flattering or patronizing, he tactfully complimented her skilled piano playing. "That was one of the finest Chopins I've ever heard; quite an emotional approach. I sensed controlled aggressiveness and fiery excitement," Renzo said, happy to have been able to string together so many words in French.

"Well!" she said. They both stood next to the table, and she looked at him with her intense, almost burning eyes. "I didn't know that Italy has sent music critics along with all the murderers and marauders."

The impact of her brash hostility jarred Renzo. His mouth fell open. He couldn't believe such harsh words came from the same lips that recited prayers in church—the same lips that he had yearned to kiss. Renzo regained his composure and managed to respond after her stinging words sank in. "I'm sorry to see that your opinion of us is so negative. Perhaps you have heard some false propaganda."

"False?" she asked in a voice that showed a definite sign of agitation. "What if I show you otherwise?" She uttered a hearty, sarcastic laugh as she turned and darted to the adjoining room, leaving Renzo alone. He sat, poured some wine, took a sip, and tore a piece of bread.

She came back quickly, brandishing old newspaper clippings, which she contemptuously dropped on the table in front of Renzo. She tossed her jet-black tresses and lifted her chin in indignation, her face chalk white. "Propaganda, you think? Here, read this," she said in a harsh, severe tone.

The headlines were clear. One, dated June 17, 1940, read "ITALIAN AIRPLANES BOMB THE PORT OF BASTIA."

Another read "ITALIAN PLANES BOMB BORGO'S AIRPORT."

Several other clippings from more recent dates followed. One concerned the arrest of several Corsicans for possession of illegal arms. Another described a charge against the Italian police for allegedly having tortured a man named Scamaroni regarding his involvement in an attempted insurrection by the National Front against the occupying forces in December 1942. And last, there was a somewhat facetious article that accused some Italian soldiers of stealing a piglet from a Corsican farmer.

As he read he could feel her blazing eyes fixed on him. He chuckled at the piglet affair, finding it difficult to give it much credence. As for the bombings, he had no answer. He knew nothing about them. He decided to express his opinion as he saw it. "Do you think we should stay passive while these fanatic rebels conjure up all sorts of schemes to undermine our mission?" He cut a piece of lamb.

"Our patriots are no fanatic rebels."

"But that's what they are!" Renzo put his fork back on the plate, still impaling the lamb he had cut. The meal would have to wait.

She kept her eyes on him and the length and intensity of her stare told him a storm was coming his way. "What irony!" she exploded. "You have the nerve to call our patriots *rebels* for doing the same thing your rebels did in other eras. What's happened to Italy? Where are all the admirable constitutions that Count Cavour worked so hard for? Where is the democracy that Giuseppe Mazzini had preached? Where is the freedom that Giuseppe Garibaldi fought so desperately for to the last drop of his blood?"

Her passion impressed Renzo. He had no answers for her. He wanted to return to the present. He stood, feeling diminished with her standing over him. "What do they have to do with us now?" he asked.

"Well, they have done for Italy what our patriots want to do for us now—to liberate our land from the oppression of foreigners."

"But those people were highly polished intellectual leaders and noblemen," he said.

"Is freedom, then, a luxury to be achieved and enjoyed only by noblemen? I must remind you that freedom belongs to all people, including our shepherds, our peasants, and our fishermen."

Renzo could readily see that what he had hoped would be a pleasant interlude had become a fencing contest, and she seemed to have the advantage. He couldn't deny the fact that she was right. What weapon could he use to contradict her? He couldn't disagree with her and could only imagine how it felt to have another country seize your country.

"Well," he said, reaching for his glass of wine. "Those were different times. No one can bring back the Italy of one hundred years ago—years that could well have been the best for Italy."

"Yes, now you have Mussolini," she said. "Now you have your Duce, who is leading Italy to its own destruction."

Her voice was calculating and penetrating. His mind went back to the church where he had seen her kneeling in prayer. *This isn't the same woman.* The transformation was overwhelming.

There was a moment when Tonelli's words—that she "would just as soon spit in your face"—rang ominously in Renzo's ears. Her violent attack left him completely disarmed, almost impotent. He wasn't prepared for this. Slowly, he realized that her outrage was not intended as a personal attack but was the honest—though animated—expression of resentment of a woman whose rights had been violated. He knew that his response would either fuel her nationalistic pride or soothe her.

"I see you are well informed about my fatherland," he said, putting the glass back on the table and reaching for a napkin to dab his lips.

"Well, you are aware that Italy was France's sister nation, having the same interests and sharing the same ambitions until May 1939." She was pacing, animatedly waving her arms as she spoke. "But then your Duce, lured by the power of Hitler, who gave him a false illusion of strength, signed the Pact of Steel. And one year later, Mussolini stabbed France in its back, saying, 'The sisterhood has ended' and then declared war on France. Remember that? Well, where is Italy now? What has Italy done since then? Can you still shout 'Viva Il Duce'?" She had now crossed the boundary into a territory that Renzo didn't want to enter—Italian politics.

"I must remind you that I am a soldier of the Italian army. I am not a Blackshirt," Renzo said in his defense.

"But you are one of the eight million bayonets Mussolini is bragging about so much. Aren't you?"

"I owe my allegiance to the king."

"And what is your king, anyway? Just a figurehead with no authority who's only allowed to review parades, to visit wounded soldiers in hospitals, and to play with his precious collections of stamps and coins. The Duce is your master."

Renzo decided to restrain himself from any reaction. He found himself at a loss. He had wanted so desperately to influence her, but obviously, she convincingly succeeded in influencing him. All her rectitude, all her boldness had not discouraged him. Rather, she had reenergized and stimulated his spirit.

She had now given him another reason to be fascinated by her; he found himself having great respect for a woman who would not retreat. The unexpectedly long confrontation, however, left dinner untouched. Renzo glanced at the lamb roast in front of him, wondering how it tasted. It had already lost its appeal. A patina of congealed fat had formed around the meat, and it was no longer appetizing. The wine, however, with its sparkling crimson color, was still inviting.

Renzo reached for the bottle and slowly refilled the glass. With his eyes on her, he raised the glass in her direction. "*A votre santé*," he said. "I want to make a toast and a promise that I will return to visit Corsica again, someday, under better circumstances."

"Why would you want to come back here?" she asked.

"Because it is a beautiful island. In spite of the current circumstances, I find it appealing."

She cocked her head defiantly. "Well! Enjoy your stay. It will be a short one, I'm sure. You may like Corsica, but Corsica doesn't like you!"

He was aghast at that remark but tried to remain calm—even though he felt she had a dagger in her hands and was taking sadistic pleasure in twisting it in his heart. "What makes you say that?" he asked.

"How can Corsica be appealing to you? Our citizens may tolerate you, but you're neither accepted nor welcome. Was there a welcoming committee to greet you when you came? Was there a parade in your honor? No!" She crossed her arms on her chest. "But there will be a great parade when you leave. Hopefully, it will be soon."

Those last words curdled Renzo's blood. Untamable fire glowed in her eyes. For a moment, he was tempted to remind her of the reason he was there, but his determination to create a favorable impression was much stronger than the pride of a man and a soldier.

"Am I the cause of your rancor?" he asked.

"No. You're not. It's your captain's presence in this house that disturbs me. We have lost our privacy. It's the presence of your troops on our island that disturbs me. Our street lamps can no longer be lighted, and no light should be seen out of our windows after a certain hour. We have lost our freedom. We are prisoners in our own land. You have shamefully broken the armistice pact. You have violated the clause in which you agreed to 'leave all unoccupied French territory free from Axis occupation.'"

"True," he replied, "but the Vichy regime of Marshal Petain has approved this action."

"We will deal with Marshal Petain and the Vichy regime in due time," she said.

"We're not here to disrupt your life," Renzo said. "We're not here to tamper with your social and economic affairs. You still have your civil authorities, and you still have your privacy, but it is in our interest to know what happens on the island. We're not here to harm you."

"What are you here for, then?"

"To protect you from the Allied forces."

"Ah! Who's going to protect us from you? We can protect ourselves. Our history will someday prove that you are like a bad case of measles or mumps. There is nothing you can do to prevent them. You patiently tolerate them and wait until they disappear. So, you, too, will someday disappear without leaving any scars. You have come in the dark of night, and in the dark of night you will go away, leaving no trace."

She was silent now, her eyes moist, and Renzo tried to come to grips with the situation. He looked at her intently, and he realized there were two things that needed to be treated with care—fragile things and explosive things. And it was clear to him that she was a little bit of both.

Sensing she had exhausted her apparent anger, Renzo stood directly in front of her, looking into her eyes. Her arms were crossed in front of her, maintaining her defiant attitude. It occurred to him that not only was she unaware of his feelings for her but that they were on opposing sides, pitted against one another by a war that neither had asked for.

"We are both victims of the times," he whispered. "We didn't start this war, and we are not responsible for the rift that exists between our nations. Our leaders should be blamed and chastised, not us." Her black, smoldering eyes were now clear and calm, almost pleading. She braved a smile with the hint of reconciliation, while a tear slid down her cheek and onto her white angora vest.

Renzo looked deeply into her eyes. "Let us treat each other as humans and not as Nazis or Fascists or Maquisards. Can't we rid ourselves of all this resentment and hate? That's all we can do to keep our sanity in the middle of this insanity." He had nothing more to add and remained silent. All was quiet, except for the barely audible sound of the grandfather clock in the receiving room. "Wars are terrible," Renzo said, breaking the tension. "They are nothing but insults to history."

She looked at him attentively, and it seemed as if his words had suddenly begun to melt the iceberg that encased her. A flicker of a smile appeared on her lips, and it soon blossomed into a full grin. She lowered her arms and left them hanging at her side, somewhat limp. She bowed her head slightly and fixed her eyes on the red Abyssinian cat that had been in the corner of the room all the while, dozing. "I'm sorry to have spoiled your dinner," she said, looking back at Renzo, her anger subsiding. "There wasn't any reason to attack you so unjustly." She was pensive for a second and then said, "I don't know. Perhaps it's your uniform that makes me cringe, or maybe it's the sound of those boots that remind me of the Nazis, but please ... forgive me. I just got carried away."

She seemed to be genuinely contrite, and Renzo was certain that she had finally realized that he was not responsible for the war.

Their conversation had been so engrossing and thought-provoking that neither of them was aware of the time. They were left in the kitchen, surrounded by a soothing darkness. The kerosene lamp was empty. Only the flickering light of a candle burning under a large crucifix on the wall kept them from complete darkness. She reached for a tin can of kerosene and began to fill the crystal lamp.

Renzo held the lamp for her while she poured, and for an instant, his fingertips touched hers. They looked into each other's eyes, and he could see a puzzled look in hers. The hard lines on her lips had disappeared and a slight smile had taken its place.

"So, you like Chopin?" she asked. Her voice was now calmer.

"Yes. I like Chopin immensely."

"Do you have any favorites?"

"Yes. I'm very fond of his scherzi, especially the third."

"I'm familiar with it but only vaguely. I haven't been able to master it yet. Chopin's repertory is so vast, and my knowledge is so limited. Maybe someday I will," she concluded, wistfully.

Renzo had been looking for some way to improve the tone of their conversation and was happy to see that it was she who found the way. They returned to the initial subject—music—but realizing the time, he thought it would be best to continue the conversation another day, possibly at dinner the following evening. Although he didn't have the desire to leave, he also didn't have the courage to stay.

It had been a long and eye-opening evening. Renzo had learned a great deal about the young lady. She was well educated and well informed and certainly not afraid to speak her mind. He saw, in her, courage, strength, and loyalty. There was not a trace of ostentation in her attitude, and above all, there was a complete lack of hypocrisy that made him admire her even more. He felt proud to see that, in a world so shamefully saturated with hate, all these noble qualities still existed.

Reluctantly, he prepared to leave, and he reached for his first-aid kit. They walked toward the front door together.

"Forgive my rudeness," she said coyly. "I don't know what came over me. I didn't intend to carry on that way. Please forgive me, Renzo."

At the mention of his name, his heart swelled. He was no longer *Monsieur le soldat* but Renzo—a human being.

She opened the door with one hand while still holding the kerosene lamp in the other. As she stretched her arm out of the door to light his way, a gust of wind came rolling around the house, blowing out the lamp's flame. Renzo turned around. She was so close to him; her face was so near that their cheeks almost touched. Renzo wanted to kiss her, but a voice inside suggested not to. Instead, he reached for her free hand and kissed her fingers gently and with a passionate tenderness. She looked at him with a questioning glance but said nothing.

"I still don't know your name," he said.

"Adrienne," she said. "Adrienne Santi."

Immediately, he felt a lump of tenderness in his parched throat. She was no longer an abstract stranger to him. Not simply "the lady in the tailored, pale blue suit" but Adrienne, the woman he had his sights on for so long.

"Thank you, Adrienne. Good night," he whispered.

"*Bona notte,*" she answered in her charming Corsican dialect.

"Keep Grandmama comfortable," he urged her. "I'll return tomorrow."

She nodded quietly and smiled.

When the door closed behind him, he remained there, alone and spellbound. He sat for a while on the bottom step of the cozy porch, admiring the wondrous splendor of the night. Myriad stars that seemed near enough to grab glimmered in the clear sky. The moon, with a wide orange hue around it, stood high above. The air was filled with the intoxicating aroma of wildflowers, mixed with the salty scent of the sea that rose from the valley down below.

He lingered there, unconscious of the time, feeling renewed and purified. "Adrienne. Adrienne!" he whispered to himself. The very sound of her name gladdened his heart. He felt like the happiest man in the troubled world. He wondered how the events of the evening had affected her. He wished he could be a fly on the wall and see her reaction. Although Adrienne's feelings were a mystery, Renzo left the house with the opposite feeling from when he first approached the front door. He had gone there disinterested, almost unwilling and somewhat annoyed, and he had left elated and grateful for having been asked to go. He wished he could have stayed longer to continue their conversation, but he knew one thing—there was still tomorrow.

7 *Dinner with the Santis*

Tonelli had accompanied Nino to General Headquarters to escort Captain Benelli, so the following day Renzo had no one to speak with about the previous evening's events. His day progressed as usual, and as he tended to all his pressing duties in the infirmary, he felt exhaustion slowly taking hold of him.

Yet when evening fell and he climbed the road to the Santis' house, he was stimulated by the idea that he would see Adrienne again and felt renewed and invigorated. Unlike the past evening, when he had climbed the same road feeling downcast and with his eyes to the ground, his head now was clear, his spirit high, and his eyes more alert. That alertness gave him a chance to admire the Santis' house more closely.

Although an aura of importance surrounded it, there was no sign of isolation from the other nearby houses. Contrarily, it seemed that each cobblestone along the road was a connecting link that tied it to the rest of the village below. The Santis' house appeared to be a symbol of strength in an occupied but undefeated island.

Renzo didn't know what to expect, but from the moment he stepped on the front stoop he felt that it would be a pleasant evening. For one thing, he didn't need to knock three times. Just as he lifted the lion's head, Adrienne opened the door.

Her greeting was brief but pleasant. "Please come in," she simply said in a soft voice. "Grandpapa and Grandmama are also waiting for you."

The word "also" boosted his confidence. It must have meant

that she, too, had been waiting for him, but there was no time for supposition. As he entered the house, Monsieur Santi approached the door to greet him. Yet, however pleasant a sight that was, Renzo was overcome by a sense of intimidation. Monsieur Santi wasn't an imposing figure, but Renzo realized the man standing in front of him was the grandfather of the woman with whom he had fallen in love.

Monsieur Santi, a man in his sixties, walked with a firm, assured step, similar to that of a confident, young, and well-trained athlete. With an open smile, he extended his arms and then pumped Renzo's hand with one of his, while holding his elbow with the other. His hand clasp was sure and unhurried, but as his hand touched Renzo's, the young soldier felt as if an icy blanket had been thrown over him. He couldn't understand the reason for this sudden chill or why shivers ran up and down his spine.

Monsieur Santi, a man of medium stature, appeared calm and relaxed. A round head covered with a thick mane of white hair domed a rugged, deeply bronzed, almost leathery face. In striking contrast, a thick set of black eyebrows, arching above a pair of deep-set, piercing black eyes, dominated his gentlemanly, aristocratic figure. His fashionable, casual clothes clearly indicated that he was in full control of his house—brown corduroy coat, open-collared white shirt with a loosely tied black cravat, brown flannel slacks, and brown shoes. To Renzo, that was a clear sign that the man had neither the intention to impress nor the need to prove anything to anybody.

Renzo had dressed carefully and fastidiously. For this special occasion, he wore his best uniform—not just to make a favorable impression but also not to create a negative one.

"Welcome to our house," Monsieur Santi said. "It's good to meet you, Renzo."

"It's good to meet you, too, Monsieur. And thank you for your invitation. It's an honor to accept it."

As the three stood just inside the doorway, Monsieur Santi looked at Renzo from head to toe and openly smiled again. Renzo could plainly see he was under scrutiny. "I see you have broken your law," Monsieur Santi remarked, pointing at Renzo's waist, obviously noticing he wasn't carrying his sidearm. "You are also defying the many dangers that could arise around here at night," he continued.

"It feels good to disobey orders sometimes. It makes one feel free, Monsieur," Renzo said. "As for the dangers, I'll take my risks. I've been invited to your home as a friend. I've come to your home as a friend, and as far as I know, a friend never carries guns into a friend's home."

"Commendable attitude," Monsieur Santi praised. "Please come in." That cordial welcome made the chills vanish, and Renzo felt as if he were being showered with pure Corsican hospitality. "Thank you for having come so promptly last evening and on such short notice," he continued, his voice sincerely solemn. "And for being so kind to Madame Santi."

"Oh, I'm only too glad to have been of help. I'm very happy that it wasn't a more severe accident. She would've needed a doctor."

"This is a strange irony, though, Renzo," Monsieur Santi said, shaking his head. "This district has produced, by percentage, more doctors than any other region in Corsica, but there aren't many of them around. It seems that once they have finished their internship in their local hospitals, they immigrate to mainland France and never come back, except for vacation."

"And how's Madame Santi this evening, Monsieur?"

"She's doing fine. Come, see for yourself."

Monsieur Santi led Adrienne and Renzo into the spacious great room where Adrienne had played the piano the previous night. Madame Santi was comfortably seated on a large, stuffed red armchair, looking well rested. Her legs were on top of a red ottoman, and she wearing both shoes.

During the night, as Renzo expected, the swelling of her ankle had gone down, and the bandages had loosened enough that she had been able to remove them herself.

"I'm happy to see you out of bed and looking so well, Madame. May I take a look?" Renzo pointed at her ankle.

"Certainly," she replied.

Renzo knelt in front of her and quickly examined her. "Good, very good," he commented. "The rock garden is waiting for you!"

"Come with me now, Renzo," interrupted Monsieur Santi. "I'll show you the house. Domenica still has work to do on dinner."

Domenica was an old woman, who, Monsieur Santi explained,

was a neighbor who had been with the Santi family for many years, filling many positions—baby-sitting for Adrienne since her birth, cleaning woman, cook, as well as water fetcher and confidant.

Monsieur Santi led Renzo through the great room, where, along with the piano, many seats, and a large sofa, there was a sizeable marble bust of Napoleon resting majestically on a round cast-iron stand. Framed paintings of the "Little Corporal" lined the walls. Although the decor of the room was more like a shrine than a room for people to enjoy life, it impressed Renzo. But when Monsieur Santi, brimming with pride and confidence, escorted Renzo into his library, Renzo was impressed even more. A vast collection of memorabilia, worthy of a museum, was on display. On one wall hung a series of nineteenth-century tribal Berber flintlock rifles with brass and metal decoration on their stocks, together with a pair of flintlock pistols beautifully detailed with ivory inlaid stocks. On another wall, flanking both sides of a life-sized painting of Napoleon, were two antique Spanish cavalry swords.

Joined at the corners of the other two walls stood several shelves filled with books by all sorts of authors—French, Italian, English, and even German. Above the shelves was a neatly hung series of lithographs of Corsican panoramas. Four plush chairs surrounded a massive ebony desk, which occupied most of the floor space.

Monsieur Santi was very talkative and incredibly knowledgeable, and judging from the size and diversity of his book collection, it was obvious why. Renzo was sure those books weren't there simply to occupy space.

"We had abnormally hot weather last summer and autumn," Monsieur Santi continued, motioning Renzo to take one of the seats as he walked to his chair behind the desk. "I believe it has caused something to go awry with the poultry in the area. The hens are laying fewer eggs, the farmers have insufficient crops and, due to the drought, there isn't enough pasture for the sheep. That has created a shortage of milk and a scarcity of cheese. But worst of all, now, with all those German ships cruising on Corsican water, the local fishermen can't find any fish. You may not be aware, but the German authority has even prohibited the hunting of rabbits, birds, and wild pigs. There is a Nazi decree, ordering that any firearms owned by civilians, whether used for hunting or defense, should be confiscated and destroyed."

There was no exaggeration in his statement. Renzo had heard of some of these abuses by the Germans against the Corsican people, but the occupying forces from Italy had no interest in intervening on their behalf.

"And you see how it is, dear Renzo," he concluded in a voice that vibrated with drama, "any Corsican deprived of his gun feels like a eunuch in a crowded harem."

The effusive, passionate disdain for the Germans that Monsieur Santi had unashamedly professed was in such a strong contrast with the gentle affability he had previously shown that it caused some uneasiness to grow in Renzo.

Renzo thought Monsieur Santi might be trying to find out his own feelings about the Germans. He wasn't sure of the older man's motives and instantly, an irrational fear overtook him. He felt uneasy and strangely nervous. He decided not to give in to any suspicions, but he continued to watch Monsieur Santi who, with deliberate movements, placed a bookmark shaped like the French flag in an open book about Napoleon. Then he patted the book gently, closed it with much care, and tidily placed it on the far corner of the desk on top of a pile of other books.

"How fortunate you are, Monsieur, to have so many books at your disposal!" Renzo commented.

"Oh, yes, these are my friends, you know." He paused for a second, picked up a pipe from the top of the desk, filled it with tobacco, pressed it down with his index finger, and lighted it. "You see, we islanders tend to be loners. Oh, yes, we do have friends, but we seldom open our soul to others. We seem to be born with a sense of isolation—a sense that we deeply respect, a sense that stays with us throughout our lives. So, these books are my best friends. It is to them that I come when I'm in need of support." A slight smile crossed his tanned face.

At that moment Domenica entered the room, carrying a silver tray filled with a pyramid of sea urchins, a bottle of wine, and two crystal goblets. Setting them down on the desk, she said, "Enjoy them, gentlemen," and then left the room.

Monsieur Santi explained. "These prickly little creatures are a Corsican delicacy that are to be enjoyed slowly and must be drowned in good wine." He paused for a moment, rubbed his hands briskly, showing an anticipation of pleasure, and began to pour.

Noisily, they slurped a few sea urchins and drank a little wine with plenty of zest, and as they proceeded, Monsieur Santi became more talkative and somewhat reflective.

"It's a damned shame, though, that we are at war. Were it not for that, we could be here, in this peaceful home, without worrying of being spied on by the authorities and free from the fear of being killed in some cowardly ambush."

"Yes, it is a shame." Renzo shifted in his seat, crossing and uncrossing his legs at his ankles.

"Whose fault is it, anyway?" Monsieur Santi continued, choosing his words for maximum effect. "Who could have predicted that Benito Mussolini would dig such a deep chasm between our two nations, which, by their own nature, were meant to work together for their mutual benefit with love and respect. But somewhere Il Duce took the wrong turn. Hitler bamboozled him. With his catch phrases and double talk, Mussolini painted a glowing picture of nonexistent power on a façade of false prosperity to the Italian people, who accepted, or pretended to accept, his Fascism. Oh, yes, he has temporarily won the battle of the minds but how? Not by intellectual persuasion but by open threats, intimidation, and castor oil. Allured by the might of Hitler, he has plunged Italy into a war without ever informing his people of the real state of the nation and has kept them as blind as a litter of newborn kittens."

From time to time, Monsieur Santi would pause long enough to slurp a couple more sea urchins, drink a few sips of wine, and take a few puffs on his pipe.

Renzo followed suit, trying to enjoy the moment but finding it difficult to listen to Monsieur Santi's diatribe. He reminded himself that it was imperative to mind his manners and to be cautious in expressing any political or military opinions. His mind, however, was not on Mussolini or Hitler, and it certainly was not on the wine or the sea urchins. He was thinking about Adrienne and how sweet it would be to see her and to be near her.

But Monsieur Santi continued. "Mussolini is the devil's chaplain," he said, slapping the desk, "and as such, he has not only disgraced Italy's heritage, but he also has stripped Italy of all the vestiges of two thousand years of its glorious past."

Although Monsieur Santi had given a good sample of his knowledge, Renzo knew he should be prepared for more. Monsieur Santi narrowed his eyes in a long, empty stare, as if in deep concentration. He furrowed his brow and for a second seemed to be rummaging in his mind for the exact words to say. Then, rubbing his chin, he continued. "Some of you, young and old, have been caught in the web that Fascism has spun. Some have vowed blind obedience to Il Duce, and some others have unwillingly succumbed to an inflicted form of volunteerism. Many people have been influenced by his catch phrase, 'It's better to live one day as a lion than a hundred years as a sheep!' But as I see it, his day is almost over. This is his sunset. Mussolini may think that Hitler will protect him and will treat him as an equal, but little does Il Duce know that Hitler wants to be his master. The marriage of Rome and the Third Reich will be an unfortunate one. The stronger Nazis will surely emerge as the dominating force."

Suddenly Monsieur Santi's face became sullen. He squinted so intensely that Renzo could see a little network of tiny furrows forming around his eyes. His evenly arched black eyebrows had moved so close together that they appeared to have become one. "I sincerely doubt the ability of this tremendously talented sorcerer to keep the people's emotions wound up much longer. The bubble of mass illusion will soon burst and then, nothing but vacuum will remain for the unfortunate Italian people. The hope that appeared on the face of Italy on the day he declared himself Il Duce has become a malignant mass. It is up to the Italian people to remove it quickly, before it's too late. It is Mussolini who's keeping Italy all puckered up, waiting for the kiss of a better life, but all they will get is the kiss of death. Fascism is doomed to a total humiliating defeat." His tone of voice progressed from the gentle tone of a grammar school teacher to the sound of a roaring earthquake. After a brief pause, he folded his arms and leaned back in his chair. "What do you think, Renzo? Do you agree with me?"

Renzo said nothing. He remembered the admonition of his grandfather, who had often told him, "It's good to know when to speak, but it's better to know when to stay silent." And silent he decided to remain. "I'm listening, Monsieur. I'm listening. You certainly have some strong opinions."

The older gentleman's professional manner had tremendously impressed Renzo. He had such self-assurance and confidence that Renzo felt nothing but awesome respect. He was a profoundly educated man with a forceful personality—an engaging conversationalist.

"What a pity," Monsieur Santi resumed after sucking down another sea urchin. "A nation that once was the cradle of civilization, whose scholars, innovators, and legislators had electrified the world with their political, military, and ethics ideas has been reduced to nothing. And all for one man—Benito Mussolini." His eyes clouded temporarily but he quickly continued. "Mussolini has been tricked by Hitler's promising him equal status in the Axis, but all he wanted was to toss Italy against France, to use the Italian fleet and its blind collaboration in order to balance the scale of power in Europe, which resulted in Italy's being banned from the League of Nations and having sanctions imposed on her. Fate is against Italy. Hitler will never win. And even if he does, Italy would still be the loser. Hitler would be the leader; Mussolini will remain his orderly."

Once again he paused and reached for the remaining sea urchins and the nearly empty bottle, and together they finished both. Then Monsieur Santi's flashing eyes shifted impatiently around the room. He looked at Renzo and continued his dissertation. "Italy was not prepared for this war. Its armed forces are still weary from the Abyssinian campaign and its intervention in the Spanish war. The crucial battle of Greece had been lost, and so were the battles of Albania and Croatia. Italy can never win this war. Oh, yes, Mussolini, in his pep talks, boasts about having eight million bayonets, but bayonets alone don't win wars. Italy is fighting with inadequate, rusted, antiquated weapons, relics of the old war. What Italy needs are a modern cache of weapons and a vast supply of modern equipment, but Italy has none. The only thing that's left is the Italian Navy. It's new and strong but for lack of fuel, it can't roam the seas. What good is a navy anchored at port?"

He turned his palms up and spread his arms apart, indicating the answer should be obvious, and then continued. "What has happened to the wisdom of the Italians to have allowed such an alliance with the Germans? Apparently, they have forgotten the old saying 'Where Germans are, Italians will never be.' But Mussolini, like a puppet in the hands of a crafty master puppeteer, is obeying faithfully all of Hitler's commands and is dancing faster and faster, like a mechanical doll, to the music of the German piper. He has confused and brainwashed the Italian youth, locking up their minds and throwing away the keys."

At that point, for the first time, Renzo felt the need to speak. "Perhaps Il Duce has locked up our lips, Monsieur, but not our minds. My tongue may not speak words of freedom now, but certainly, I have not lost the grasp of its meaning."

"You agree with me, then, Renzo?"

"I believe it prudent to just listen."

"Just remember, Renzo. The Hitler regime might appear to be your protector, but that's only a mask. In reality, the Führer will be your master. He began his dominance of Italy by first sending Germans as consultants and advisers. Little by little, they took control of all the major military bases and all the centers of communication until they achieved sole possession of the entire Italian peninsula."

It surely had been a stimulating conversation—although it actually felt like a long sermon—but unlike the emotional lashing Renzo had received from Adrienne the previous evening, this had underlined, with more clarity, all that surrounded Renzo's life at the moment. He felt that Monsieur Santi was not debating him but that, in effect, he had given a lesson in political science and a careful analysis of Italy's tangled situation—or perhaps a preview of history that was yet to be written. With his logic and effective oratory, Monsieur Santi had dissected the economic, political, military, and historic structure of Italy and its government, showing Renzo all the cancerous blemishes on its skin, the atrophy of its muscles, and the cracks in its bones. Monsieur Santi had come to the conclusion that unless Italy got rid of Mussolini, Italy could never join the family of free nations.

It was strange, considering the short time Renzo had spent with him, but he had developed a sincere liking and admiration for this erudite Corsican, who in essence was his enemy.

What had amazed Renzo about their conversation was the similarity of opinion that both Adrienne and Monsieur Santi shared, except that while Adrienne had flared up in a passionate, emotional reaction, Monsieur Santi's dissertation was a complete, analytical, and realistic evaluation of an historic event. Yet despite Monsieur Santi's sharp condemnation of Il Duce, Renzo realized the man liked Italy and the Italian people. He'd told Renzo he had visited Italy many times in his younger days, and each time he returned home, he had brought with him nothing but good memories.

Still, despite Renzo's positive feelings, he couldn't understand why he also had a strong feeling of unease.

Just then Domenica came in to retrieve the tray and to announce that dinner was ready. The sea urchins had not only been an unexpected surprise but a tasty appetizer as well. As they headed to the dining room, Renzo asked Monsieur Santi if he had ever had any conversation like this with Captain Benelli.

"Definitely not," he said, looking almost irked. "Your captain is nothing but a self-inflated windbag and a loud charlatan with nothing in his skull but gonads instead of brains. He's a self-centered fanatic, interested only in what he has to say. He bores me tremendously."

Such a prompt assessment almost made Renzo laugh out loud. He had to admire Monsieur Santi's candor. Renzo didn't know anyone who had ever dared to speak that way about Captain Giancarlo Maria Francesco Benelli.

****

As they entered the dining room, Renzo could sense a distinct air of aristocracy bouncing off every wall. An immense fireplace was the most prominent feature in the room. On the center of its wide mantelpiece, a round golden clock inside a square ebony case ticked the minutes away. On either end of the mantelpiece stood two stunning marble stallions, one white and one black, facing each other with their front legs high in the air, as if engaged in a fight to the death. A round dining table occupied the center of the room. It was covered with a festive, colored linen cloth and filled with all sorts of Corsican delicacies.

Madame Santi and Adrienne were seated, waiting for them. Monsieur Santi, with patrician countenance, filled the four goblets with his fine new wine. Still standing, he raised his glass, swished it around a few times, and looked at the legs forming against the bright light of the kerosene lamp that hung from the ceiling.

"I want to make a toast!" he said in a solemn tone. "I drink to your health and to your honor, Renzo."

"And I to yours, Monsieur!" Renzo replied.

"I drink to the honor of your family!"

"Thank you, Monsieur. And I to yours," Renzo echoed.

"I drink to the honor of your country!"

"My country?" Renzo asked, somewhat surprised.

"Yes, your country!" Monsieur Santi staunchly affirmed. "I wish you no ill. Yes, except for one man, I drink to the honor of your country."

"And I to yours!"

"Wait, wait," Monsieur Santi urged as they were about to bring the glasses to their lips. "I want to say something to you all." He raised his glass and in a theatric gesture said, "Fill the glass that is empty. Empty the glass that is full. Never leave it empty, and never leave it full!"

Renzo raised his glass to each of them, wanting to say something clever, but he could only manage to say, "I wish you peace."

Madame Santi politely drank to Renzo's family and future. When Renzo pointed his glass in Adrienne's direction, his eyes fixed on hers as he repeated the words he had said to her the evening before: *"A votre santé, mademoiselle."*

She said nothing, but Renzo noticed a Mona Lisa smile form on her impeccably shaped lips. It wasn't a smile of invitation, but he could sense it was a sincere smile, devoid of any fake acceptance. He hoped the smile indicated a new start in their relationship.

Renzo savored the plentiful meal set before him and followed Monsieur Santi's suggestion—Santi never left Renzo's glass empty, and Renzo never left it full. As the time rolled by and the food disappeared, Renzo felt a special kind of warmth in the house—not the warmth that came from the good Cape Corse wine he had enjoyed all evening but the warmth of friendliness that he'd forgotten existed. Renzo also was elated at the turn of events regarding Adrienne in the past forty-eight hours—from searching for her, to unexpectedly finding her at the Santis' home, to their heated discussion, and then finally a rapprochement of sorts.

As much as Renzo would have liked to stay longer, a look at the clock made him realize that he shouldn't abuse their hospitality. It was time to return to La Grande Maison. When he made an attempt to rise, Madame Santi insisted he should remain a little longer.

"Adrienne will regale us with a little music," she said. "Won't you, *ma chérie?*" she added, looking at Adrienne.

Adrienne nodded.

Renzo had hoped he would have another opportunity to hear her play and was excited at the announcement. They moved to the living room, where the Santis settled into a plush, tan Chesterfield sofa. Monsieur Santi motioned for Renzo to sit in a similarly upholstered wingback chair that was near the sofa. Adrienne went to the piano. She sat quietly, resting her hands on the keyboard. She remained motionless. Renzo thought at first that this hesitation was part of her personal routine, but it wasn't so. He realized his error when he heard the noise of the unwinding springs and the chimes of the clock on the mantelpiece. Ten o'clock. That was what she was waiting for.

She smiled lightly and bowed her head in jest to the clock, as if to give it a gracious thank-you, knowing it now would not interfere with the sound of her playing. She struck the first note, and at that moment, Renzo's spirit soared. He recognized the piece instantly—Chopin's Scherzo #3 in C-sharp Minor; the same scherzo he'd mentioned to her the previous evening. Renzo watched ecstatically as her slim fingers glided gracefully up and down the keyboard, producing a beautiful sound.

Renzo glanced at the elder Santis to see if they were accepting the scherzo in the same way as he was. Madame Santi was enthralled, sitting on the couch with her hands clutching the silver-handle cane, and her chin leaning on it. A serene exhilaration settled in her eyes.

A glow of pride and a grin of satisfaction covered Monsieur Santi's face as he sat alongside Madame Santi, his feet crossed one on top of the other, and his hands folded across his abdomen, like a contented bishop.

Renzo saw Domenica standing by the kitchen, leaning against the doorframe with her hands folded beneath her apron. She had a sweet, contemplative smile of admiration that had made all the wrinkles on her face disappear. She seemed to be more proud of Adrienne than anyone else in the room.

At one point, Madame Santi leaned toward Renzo as if she wanted to share a big secret. "She practiced it all day long, you know," she said.

That welcome news was another boost to his spirits. He remained silent, holding his breath, studying all the subtleties of Adrienne's facial expressions, which ranged from an intense look in her eyes to a serene state of deep concentration. As he watched, he felt a growing love for her, yet he wondered how many sides to Adrienne there were. He had seen her angelic, spiritual side in church; he'd witnessed her determined, idealistic side in the kitchen; and now he watched, in awe, an accomplished, talented artist at her best. *Was there another side to her?*

When the scherzo ended and she folded her hands over her lap, Monsieur Santi applauded and shouted "Brava" with such glee and leaped off his chair so fast that his pipe slipped out of his mouth, falling on the floor with a clattering bang.

****

It had been a superb evening, one of those evenings Renzo knew he would remember forever. The Santis' hospitality had been impressive, the dinner succulent and delicious, and the wine excellent. Domenica had been polite and respectful; Adrienne's recital, inspiring; and the outpouring of Monsieur Santi, lively and stimulating.

Once again, Madame Santi thanked Renzo profusely for his assistance. As he stood to leave she gave him an open invitation. "Please come and see us again, any time!"

Monsieur Santi shook Renzo's hand and patted him on the shoulder, and for some reason, another shiver crawled like a snake down Renzo's spine. "I haven't had such an interesting conversation in a long time," Santi said.

"It's been a pleasure, I assure you. And once again, thank you for your gracious hospitality," Renzo replied.

Adrienne escorted Renzo to the door.

"Thank you for the scherzo," Renzo said. "It soothed my heart."

"I dedicated it to you as a peace offering," she said. "I know that I was rude and mean. Could you ever forgive me for the hurt I inflicted on you last evening?"

Renzo slowed his steps and boldly turned around, facing her, his eyes firmly focused on hers. "There's no need of forgiveness," he said. "I admire and respect the feelings you have for your country. I can't condemn you for it, because that's the way I feel about my country. But if you want to offer me an apology for personal redemption, would you consider seeing me … alone?"

She stopped at the door, looking surprised. Renzo saw her brow furrow, but as she spoke there was no hesitation in her voice. "Are you at liberty to take time out from your duty?"

Renzo's heart was in his throat. "Occasionally."

"Well," she said, "there is a rarely traveled trail that begins directly behind the church. Follow it until you reach a large granite boulder. There, the trail divides in two. Take the one on the right and continue until you find a natural grotto. I go there every morning about nine o'clock. Wait there for me."

"When?"

"Tomorrow or any other day."

He felt as if he was in one of his dreams—and at last one would come true. All he could say was, "I'll be there tomorrow."

8 *Meeting at the Grotto*

Tonelli's responsibilities were completed, and he returned from General Headquarters while the captain and Nino remained. Renzo brought him up to date about the last two nights. He knew he could trust Tonelli. He wasn't concerned about admitting that he would be violating the fraternization policy. Renzo told Tonelli he was on his way to his first rendezvous with Adrienne.

"So, you've finally met your angel. And she played a piece on the piano especially for you!" Tonelli teased. "Maybe I should take my guitar to the house and perform a duet with her."

"She's much too refined for a man like you, Alvaro," Renzo shot back, while straightening his uniform. "And I doubt she'd be interested in the type of duet you'd want to play."

"Believe me, I was talking about music, but I'm available for duets of any kind when a beautiful woman is concerned." Tonelli placed both hands on Renzo's shoulders and looked him in the eye. "I can tell you're a bit tense about seeing her today." He rubbed Renzo's shoulders and then patted him on both cheeks. "Calm down; she's only a woman."

"A very special woman, Tonelli. I hope you have a chance to meet someone like her someday." He paused and looked thoughtfully at Tonelli. "I'm going to need you more than ever."

"How?"

"If this all develops as I would like, I hope to see her often. That would mean some unexplained and unauthorized absences from my post."

"Renzo, you're a dedicated soldier. You wouldn't leave if there were a real need for you to be here. If any questions come up, I'll take care of it. I've talked my way out of many tough situations at home. I'm sure I can do it here."

"You're a good friend, Alvaro. Thank you." Renzo grabbed his cap and left the infirmary.

****

Renzo's high nervousness over meeting Adrienne had scaled to new heights when Lieutenant Boschetto spotted him. The lieutenant was standing by the door, keeping an observant eye on the potato-peeling cook, and Renzo had tried to sneak past him, unnoticed.

Lieutenant Orazio Boschetto sported a big handlebar mustache and an out-of-regulation long crop of hair that was plastered down with brilliantine. He looked like an owl that had fallen into a jar of olive oil. The unctuous officer's vanity caused him to spend an unusual amount of time combing his hair and grooming his mustache. In a methodic routine, he would obsessively remove his helmet and comb his hair every chance he had. "Where are you going all dressed up—to meet the Pope?" he asked.

Renzo had no plausible response to that unexpected question, but fortunately, aware as he was of the lieutenant's obsession, an inspired idea came to him. To avoid giving a response, he feigned concern for the lieutenant's appearance and asked, "What's happened to your mustache, sir?"

"Why? What's the matter with it?" he asked, alarmed, patting it nervously with his fingers.

"I don't really know, sir, but you should take a look at it for yourself." Renzo amazed himself with his newfound wit, but couldn't pat himself on the back yet; he had no time for that. He didn't know what the lieutenant's reaction would be, once he discovered his mustache was impeccable. Renzo watched as the lieutenant rushed to his quarters to consult with his mirror. Once the lieutenant was out of sight, Renzo continued on his way.

He had no trouble finding the rock that Adrienne had mentioned. He had, in fact, passed by it many times, but it was so well hidden that he'd never noticed or explored what was behind what seemed to be a natural, high, thick fence of flowering vines, just a few meters from the roadside.

The sun shone brightly and a soft breeze from the south mingled with a subtle but steady aroma of wildflowers in bloom. Almost spring, the temperature had noticeably risen, and giant, shaggy clouds wandered leisurely across the deep-blue sky. A light mist hugged the rugged coastline below, while the dew that covered the path ahead remained undisturbed, as if no one had gone over it yet. That gladdened him. It was an indication that he would be the one to wait.

As Renzo entered her secret woodland, an idyllic setting opened up in front of him. An endless mixture of wildflowers with patches of brilliant colors sprung up. He looked to the right, and out of a high, massive rock protruding from a hill streamed many little cascades. They furiously splashed down with a tumultuous sound, digging separate channels in the earth. As they merged, they formed a torrent. Like a giant silver serpent, it ran across his path. It then leaped over a high cliff and continued its bubbling journey down the hill, going through a thick grouping of plants and shrubs in full bloom.

To his left, immediately across the torrent, were myriad beautiful lilies. Farther down was a shimmering mantle of pink and pale blue lilacs and forget-me-nots, which like an infinite blanket of silk and satin, reflected the glimmering colors of the rainbow.

In the middle of the field was a huge, primitive rock, with running red veins that looked like blood and speckles of a metallic-looking substance, which shined in the sun like many tiny mirrors. It was stunning, probably dating back to prehistoric times. The elements had slowly eroded it and carved a large opening on its side, making a grotto that looked almost threatening. Its floor was covered with a luscious carpet of thick blue-green moss. Beads of water dropped down from the walls, creating a pleasant tinkling sound. Such a grotto could well have been a natural shelter for shepherds at one time—or perhaps outlaws and bandits.

From a large opening on its dome, half covered by a flat slab of shiny rock, he could see a ceiling of azure as clear and flawless as he had ever seen—the Corsican sky. Farther down, at the edge of an interminable cliff, stood the remnants of an ancient, dry-stone

Genovese tower, a structure probably built before the new civilization. It guarded the entire valley like an intimidating, stern sentinel.

The fields all around were clothed with honeysuckle and thyme. The surrounding hills were thick with pine, larch, beech, and oak trees on whose branches the birds, already ornate in their springtime plumage, were singing their mating songs.

It was a tranquility that Renzo had never experienced, and there, in this oasis of serenity filled with the calming effect of the pristine surroundings, he waited.

****

The wait wasn't long. Punctual as the morning sunrise, she appeared along a narrow path on a silver-gray bicycle. She got off the bike, cautiously leaned it against a willow tree, and then walked gracefully and confidently in Renzo's direction.

She was dressed casually; a floral printed blouse complemented a brown pleated skirt, which flowed over her knee-high socks and low-heeled brown shoes. A silk scarf of earth colors covered her head and was neatly tied under her chin. As she advanced, she removed it from her head and meticulously wrapped it over her shoulders.

Renzo took a few steps toward her, cap in hand, to greet her, but she gestured him to stay where he was. "Thank you for coming," Renzo managed to say as she stopped in front of him.

"How could I resist your plea?" she answered. "You sounded so convincing."

Renzo noticed shyness in her voice that he had not detected before. Without any fear of rejection, he reached for her hand and held it lightly. There was no reluctance on her part. The warmth of her palm encouraged him not to let go. With her hand clasped in his, they slowly walked toward the opening of the grotto.

Feeling a need to be completely open and honest, Renzo bared his soul and confessed all the events that had created such turmoil in him since Christmas. As he spoke, he felt an occasional increase of pressure on his hand, as if she wanted to pump every word out of him. When he was done, her brow furrowed slightly, and her slightly squinted eyes had an interrogative look.

"Why didn't you ever knock at our door?" she asked.

"I didn't know you were there. The captain never told me there was a young girl in your house. He's quite open with me, so I'm surprised he never mentioned you. "

"Your captain is not aware that I live in that house. He has never seen me."

"Never?"

"Never. And I'll make sure that he never will. I despise his pomposity."

"He does tend to have that characteristic; you're right. But he's a good man underneath it all."

"It must be very far beneath those layers of fat," Adrienne laughed.

"I actually knew him before the war. It's because of him that I am here now."

"Was he a family friend?"

"No. I needed an income to pay my expenses for my medical studies. I was able to get a good position at a health spa in the Adamello Mountains as an assistant to the athletic director after I took an intensive course in Swedish and sports massage. The spa mostly catered to vacationers and mountain climbers. It was there where I first met Captain Benelli. He usually spent most of his summer furloughs at the spa. I worked on him many times, and he seemed to be appreciative and pleased with my services. And then one day in January, when I was called to report to the Sant'Ambrogio Armory in Milan as a recruit, we met again. By coincidence, he happened to be the officer in charge of assignments, and without hesitation, he enlisted me in his company, where I've been ever since."

Renzo noticed that as he was speaking, his voice became stronger and his speech clearer and more vibrant. His confidence was building with every word.

"Well, maybe I just have to get used to his ways," Adrienne said, smiling coquettishly.

Standing face-to-face, they looked at each other, moving closer until their clothing almost touched. Renzo brought her hands to his lips and kissed them.

"Adrienne, now that my search for you is over, I already know I want to spend my life with you. You may think I'm being impetuous, but I know how I feel."

"Thank you, Renzo. I felt a strong attraction to you, too, once I was through ranting at you." They both laughed. "But this can't be. This shouldn't be," she said. "This is impossible. We're at war, and we're enemies." She brushed a tear from her eyes.

"That's someone else's decision," Renzo said. "That's Mussolini's and Hitler's decision, not ours. They can only tell you whom to kill and whom to maim, but they can't dictate to you whom to love."

"No, they can't," she agreed. "But we can't defy the law."

"Why not? We can if the law is faulty."

"There's a price to pay. We're not even supposed to be here together. I know that any of us caught fraternizing with any of you could face dire consequences, and I know that for the same reason, any one of you would be severely punished."

"I'd risk any punishment for you."

She glanced away for a moment and then with some hesitation, as if she didn't want to be heard, said, "How can this be? We don't even know each other." She rocked her head slowly from side to side, as if in disbelief.

"I know you well enough to realize I want to know you better. I *need* to know you better. I want you to know me better."

She looked at him, and as their eyes met again, she beamed with a beautiful smile. That smile energized him.

"I'd like to see you again," he said with renewed strength. "I'd like to know you better. I want to be part of your life as much as I need you to be part of mine."

She remained pensive for a moment and then, much to Renzo's joy, she consented.

"I don't know your schedule, nor do I know your obligations," she said. "I do come here every day at this hour." She paused briefly, as if it were painful for her to continue, and then, looking at the glistening waves lapping the shore below, she continued. "Be here whenever you are free."

"Tomorrow, then?" he said, trying to hide his enthusiasm.

She affectionately laid her hands lightly on his arms, giving him a sense of complete assurance. "Yes, tomorrow," she said.

Before she took the first step away from him, Renzo boldly extended his head toward her in search of her lips, but she demurely offered her cheek instead.

Although this was an understandable gesture from Adrienne, things were happening so fast that Renzo struggled to restrain the intense desire that was rampantly growing within him. He wanted to wrap his arms around her and hug and kiss her as he had done so many times in his dreams.

"I must caution you to be very careful in coming in or going out of here," she warned. "There are many eyes watching, and it would be a great hazard for a soldier to wander alone." She stopped for a second and then in an almost apologetic tone, she continued. "But as long as you are within these fences, you are safe. No one will dare to disturb you. This is my grandpapa's property."

Nevertheless, they realized caution was needed, and so both agreed that two things would be necessary: discretion and prudence.

With that pact, she slowly left. Enchanted, he watched her place the scarf over her head, neatly knotting it under her chin. He followed her with his eyes as she removed the bicycle from under the willow tree, mounted it, and headed for the road. When he saw her disappear beyond the last turn at the bottom of the hill, he felt desperately alone, like Adam without Eve.

9   *Building a Relationship*

enzo spent the night reliving every moment of his rendezvous with Adrienne. He had poured his heart out to her, feeling neither pain nor embarrassment. But he had placed himself in a quandary. He promised Adrienne they would meet again the next day, but he'd forgotten it was the day Captain Benelli was returning from his three-day visit to General Headquarters. Renzo had no choice. He had to stay at La Grande Maison. His lapse in memory didn't create any problems with Adrienne, and over the next few weeks they managed to meet many other times, as often as his duties permitted.

Initially, Adrienne's manner was noticeably hesitant and reserved, but eventually she began to show a growing interest in Renzo. The grotto had become more familiar to him, and he felt increasingly comfortable with Adrienne. They were able to discuss their innermost thoughts and share their aspirations, dreams, and hopes. Adrienne planned to pursue a career in music, and Renzo wanted to continue his medical studies. Neither tried to emphasize virtues or hide shortcomings—they were what they were. In time, they were able to close the chasm of national rivalry and slowly surmount the obstacles imposed on them by the war.

Their bond grew stronger with each meeting, and as time went by, they discovered that they needed each other. Their love steadily increased, as did their friendship. They were no longer separated by the war but realized that, ironically, it had been the war that brought them together.

They were so happy to occasionally spend precious time together in that magnificent oasis in the middle of a world in turmoil that they would sometimes neglect their duties. Adrienne, who had taken a volunteer job as an elementary school teacher in the village, would often have to rush to the school, pedaling furiously, and catching her breath at her desk in the classroom, to the amusement of the students. Renzo chose to forget or ignore some of his tiresome duties. No battles were being fought on the island, giving Renzo little to do in the infirmary, and his absences went unnoticed. Had it not been for the nearby sputtering sound of Nazi boats that had infested the island's coast, they would have been completely oblivious to the fact that the world was at war—and even that there was a world around them.

However, Adrienne explained to Renzo that it was because of the war that she could not tell her grandparents they were seeing each other. Although she thought her grandmother had suspicions about their budding relationship, she didn't want to confirm it. She'd heard too many rumors of the Maquisards in other areas of Corsica who made examples of women who got too close to the enemy or who allowed others to do so, and she didn't want to put her grandmother in jeopardy.

****

Three days later, Renzo managed to leave La Grande Maison and see Adrienne again. They settled down on a blanket Adrienne had brought for them. After a quick, innocent kiss, Renzo placed his hand under her chin and gently moved her head so she was looking directly into his eyes.

"I sense a little uneasiness in you this morning," he said.

"It's this war. I've been thinking about how we have to hide just to speak to each other." She placed her hands behind her to lean on them and stretched her legs out, getting comfortable. Renzo shifted to lie on his side, his head resting on the palm of his hand as he listened intently.

"Why do we need to have war?" she continued. "Not just this war now, but any war?"

"There are many reasons," he answered. "Boundary conflicts, religious zealots—"

"Maniacs like Hitler looking to take over the world."

"I was hoping we got this conversation behind us," Renzo said, looking at her with an imploring smile and tilt of his head.

"I'm sorry. You're right. But I can't help wishing for a better world, where all people can live in freedom and peace. I wish we could rid the world of all dictators, and people would all be willing to help one another and not exploit or seek domination over others. There would be no weapons and no wars. Instead of people destroying other people, people would destroy what destroys people—disease and hunger. There would be neither victors nor victims, but everyone would benefit equally—those who give assistance as well as those who receive it. Greed would be exchanged for generosity, and revenge replaced with magnanimity."

"You certainly have lofty visions for the world. I'm afraid I think there will always be people who want to exert their power and bend others to their will. And their targets will need to defend themselves if they don't want to be overtaken. Unfortunately, I think war is an inevitable evil in this world."

"When I was young, Grandpapa taught me how to hunt for pheasants, quails, and other large birds, but as I got older, I developed a growing disdain for any sort of killing and told him I no longer wanted to join him in hunting. All life is a precious gift from God, and no one should have the right to end it at will. I abhor the many deaths brought about by war."

Renzo was eager to change the subject. "Let's not talk about these things now. I want to learn more about you."

"What do you want to know?"

"Tell me about your parents."

Tears formed in the corners of Adrienne's eyes.

"I'm sorry," Renzo said, wiping a tear away with his thumb. "If it's too painful …"

"No, it's all right," she assured him but her voice quivered with sadness. "Papa was a history professor at the Sorbonne, and my mother taught music there. That's where they met. Their names were Francois and Gabrielle. They were wonderful parents. I was very close to both of them. When I was ten, they took a vacation in the Swiss Alps while I stayed here with my grandparents. One rainy day, they were traveling on a slick, tortuous, narrow road. Papa lost control of the automobile, and they plunged into a deep, rocky ravine. I was told they both died instantly. They are buried in a private grave near our small family chapel near the house. I miss them dearly."

As she spoke she looked away from Renzo, as if to hide her grief, but the purity of a child's memory was evident to him. He felt her pain, sharp and deep, as she felt it—the same way that a twin feels the pain of the sibling that is hurting. He held her in his arms for several minutes until she was composed enough to pull away.

"Thank you, Renzo. I'm fine now. I just had a thought. We are a bit like Romeo and Juliet, with one main difference."

"What's that?"

"Instead of being parts of two feuding families, we are wedged between two nations at war."

"Yes, and there are people who would be quick to judge and condemn us, if they knew we met like this."

They both were aware of being surrounded by a thousand dangers and rationally assessed what they were up against. That did not keep them from growing closer.

****

Easter passed, and May was approaching. The secret vigilance of the growing Maquisard groups increased considerably, and the possibility of Renzo and Adrienne being seen was becoming more real with every passing day. A story was confirmed of a young woman in Calvi, on the west coast, who was chased by a group of Maquisards after they heard of her indiscretion with an Italian soldier. She fell off a cliff to her death. One of the Maquisards was her brother. The soldier was never identified.

With the knowledge of stories such as this, Renzo and Adrienne realized the serious consequences they both faced if their relationship were discovered. The scandal of their clandestine love would create a burden of shame on her, together with the humiliating weight of disgrace and dishonor. It could lead to banishment for the entire family, or perhaps worse at the hands of the Maquisards. Renzo faced the possibility of a court-martial and imprisonment.

It had become increasingly risky to meet in the open air. They needed more privacy, more room, and more freedom. During their last meeting at the grotto, Adrienne proposed it would be better to rendezvous elsewhere. She suggested meeting at night at an empty hut that had once served as a place to store hay for their horses. It was located about half a kilometer from the house.

Moreover, they both realized that although they had been having a wonderful journey in their growing relationship, they still didn't know how or when they would reach the destination for which they both hungered.

10 *The Ibex Trophy*

hings weren't going well at La Grande Maison. Renzo noticed a change in Captain Benelli when he returned from his visit to General Headquarters. Renzo wondered what could possibly have happened there, other than the fact that the captain's much-anticipated promotion may have been delayed. The captain told Renzo how happy he was to have met the new commander in chief, but Renzo could detect a sense of melancholy in the captain's eyes. For one thing, it seemed strange to Renzo that with all the concern the captain had shown for Madame Santi when he'd asked Renzo to tend her ankle, he never inquired about the results of Renzo's visit to her.

It was obvious the captain had other things on his mind. He later confided in Renzo how deeply concerned he was that Italian and German intelligence discovered that the French civil and military commander, General Henri Giraud, had established contact with the Corsican patriots and slowly and secretly fomented a tide of rebellion. Some of the patriots were discovered by the Gestapo and were tortured in an attempt to gain information.

Then in April, a former high-ranking official, Colonel Paul Colonna d'Istria, a Corsican, arrived on the island. Leading the resistance movement, he succeeded in stirring, organizing, and arming the patriots, supplying them with large caches of weapons, including more than ten thousand machine guns captured by the Allies from the Germans in Tunisia. Some of these weapons came to Corsica with the French submarine *Casablanca* that was making surreptitious nightly trips from Algiers to the island. Others were parachuted onto certain predetermined places at night by British planes. The Italian military police made many arrests, and weapons were confiscated, but the danger of future deliveries was still a reality.

Because of these events, the captain became suspicious of every Corsican—men, women, and children. The men in the company were ordered to be on high alert; to report any activity they saw that was the least bit suspicious. By this point, most of the men had made attempts to at least be cordial toward the villagers and try to make themselves less of a threat to the Corsicans' normal way of life. The new orders felt like a step backward, and increased the perception that an attack by the partisans might be imminent.

The captain now exhibited severe emotional outbursts, suggesting to Renzo that all was not well with him. It was clear that the symptoms of frustration he had displayed to the shepherd shortly after their arrival had developed into a full-blown paranoia, and there had been many instances to support that opinion.

One evening, just before sunset, the captain sent Renzo and Tonelli to investigate the unusual traffic of old women going singly to a certain house and staying for unacceptably long periods of time. Two soldiers went to the house and banged on the door repeatedly until a slightly hunched-over woman let them in. After a search of the house and a half hour of questioning, their inspection proved nothing—no talks of insurrection, no plot to burn the Italian troops out of their post, no curses or evil eye cast upon them. The women were merely engaged in the recitation of the holy rosary.

On another occasion, Captain Benelli chased away a ragged young boy who was standing by the gate at dinnertime. Benelli suspected the Maquisards had sent the boy there to spy on them, but the boy pleaded that he only wanted something to eat.

Then there was the time the captain spotted a donkey laden with two bundles of dried-up branches, hoofing up the hill. A feeble, bow-legged old man followed it closely. The man, who was returning home from a day's work in the field, was hunched over to a nearly horizontal position. To ease the climb, he held on to the donkey's tail with one hand and clutched a shepherd's staff in the other. The captain personally stopped the old man and ordered him to unload the bundles. Fearing that they might contain contraband arms, the captain separated them cautiously with his riding whip. But nothing suspicious was found—only the harmless twigs the man needed to cook his evening meal.

The instability of the captain's behavior gave Renzo reason for concern. He spoke to Nino about it because Nino was in contact with him more than anyone and would have more opportunities to notice any odd behavior.

"He has been a little strange, certainly more difficult than usual," Nino said.

"In what way?"

"He asks me to do something and then as I'm doing it, he tells me to stop and says he didn't want me to do it in the first place. He seems unsure of what he wants."

"I'm concerned about him, Nino. I almost don't know who he is. Some days he seems as if he's at the threshold of losing his mind, and at other times he appears to be completely himself."

"What do you think we should do?"

Renzo hesitated. "Nothing for now, I just wanted to know what you have noticed. It's possible those quirks are intentional and simply part of an act to demonstrate he's in charge and to keep us alert." As Renzo left Nino, he held that thin thread of a positive thought. But he soon became convinced that Captain Benelli was well on his way to losing his rationality.

On a clear, windless morning, a young boy was out on the road in front of La Grande Maison, desperately trying to fly a homemade kite. He ran back and forth, over and over, until he was out of breath, but he couldn't get the kite airborne. He briefly stopped at times to rest and then would start again—only to fail once more.

Renzo kept an eye on him, admiring his perseverance, but it was painful to watch the boy's increasing frustration. Renzo remembered his own childhood with fondness and how excited he was to watch his kite soar in a limpid morning sky. For a brief moment, he wished he could relive those carefree days. And so, captured by that desire and wishing that the boy, too, could experience the same joy, Renzo approached him. "You're not running fast enough to gather the speed you need," he said. "Would you like it if I gave it a try?"

The boy handed Renzo the kite with a hopeless look in his eyes and said nothing.

Renzo tried a couple of times without success but finally, with the help of a gust of wind, the kite rose. Shaky and wobbly at first, it gradually steadied and climbed higher and higher. When it soared to incredible heights, becoming almost invisible, Renzo proudly handed it to the happy boy who, with an ear-to-ear smile of gratitude, continued to unravel the rest of the string and thanked Renzo to no end.

Just then, Renzo heard a very familiar throat-clearing sound, accompanied by the snapping of a riding whip against knee-high boots. *Il rospo*, Captain Benelli, was standing behind him with clenched fists, a stern look in his eyes, legs apart and firmly planted on the ground. Obviously not amused by Renzo's rare moment of joy, he said, "Enough of that, soldier. Do you have the same brain capacity as this boy? This isn't a playground. Show some sense and have some respect for yourself. Don't let me see you engaged in any activity like this again. Do you understand?"

Renzo was taken aback by the captain's stern reprimand. *Why would spending a moment helping a young boy, a citizen we want to have a good impression of us, be a problem?* Renzo knew he couldn't question Captain Benelli's logic. "Yes, sir. I understand." He stood at attention and saluted Captain Benelli, as did all the other soldiers milling around the yard.

The captain didn't respond to their salute. Instead, he summoned the sergeant on duty for the day and unleashed a tirade for the lack of constructive activities of the troops. "They're getting too soft and too lazy! Find something for them to do. Now!" he thundered.

"All there was to do has been done," said the sergeant. "There's nothing else for them to do at the moment, sir."

"Find something, then. And if you don't, I will!" He paused for an instant to catch his breath, his nostrils flaring like a charging bull, and then stomped briskly in an erratic pattern around the yard, like tumbleweed on a windy day. Angrily tossing his whip to the ground, he grabbed a newspaper he was carrying under his arm and furiously shredded it, throwing the pieces up in the air. They drifted all over the yard like confetti until there was nothing left in his hands but his riding whip. "Here! Now they have something to do!" he barked as he entered his office, leaving the soldiers scrambling to clean up the area.

****

Later that day the captain summoned Renzo, who, upon entering the captain's office, immediately noticed that the familiar surroundings had calmed the captain. He was sitting at his desk, which he had fastidiously arranged with everything always in its place. A calendar, inkwell, blotter, notebook, and a stemmed green goblet filled with a few pens and pencils were grouped on one side, while on the other side, objects of a personal nature were prominently displayed. Two framed photographs—individual face-on shots of his austere-looking parents—were positioned in an angle almost facing each other. Between the two photos stood a six-ringed horn of an ibex, mounted on a hoof-shaped ebony base. From what Renzo knew of the species, he believed it was from a young female, because it was relatively short—about nine inches long—and had barely any curve to it.

It was a trophy that once had belonged to Benelli's father, who had received it from the North Italian Hunting Club when the captain was still a young boy. This ibex was one of the last ones shot in Gran Paradiso National Park. Soon after, the king of Italy proclaimed the ibex an endangered species and declared its hunting illegal. The elder Benelli had given the horn to the captain as a good-luck charm, and he had treated it as such ever since.

Renzo assumed it was the captain's most cherished object. He had often seen the captain hold it fondly in one hand when faced with a problem or simply when he was in a reflective mood. He would gaze at it as if it were a precious amulet to which a deep reverence was due and also would incessantly and vigorously rub it with a piece of chamois to smooth it out and give it more luster. He had gone through this routine so many times that he had not only leveled off the six rings denoting the age of the ibex but also had given it a mirror-like finish and a needle-sharp point—like a stiletto.

The captain motioned to Renzo to take a seat. He picked up the horn and chamois to start his ritual. He smiled as he polished the horn. Renzo sat silently, watching. The captain stopped polishing for a moment, picked up an envelope, and handed it to Renzo.

"Go ahead. Open it," Benelli said, hiding any emotion and resuming the polishing process.

Renzo quickly removed the contents from the envelope. It was a letter from the Supreme Command of the Italian Forces in Italy, which in a few words denied the request of a furlough for the exams the captain had made for him. It concluded, "There will be time in the future for your exams and for a visit to your family. As for now only one thing exists—the Fatherland."

Renzo didn't know whether Captain Benelli felt sorry for him or if he was disappointed for not having been able to favorably influence the higher authorities on Renzo's behalf. The captain stopped fondling the ibex's horn and carefully returned it to the desk. Stretching his arms wide and high over his head, he looked at Renzo with disillusion on his face, as if to say, "It's out of my hands!"

Renzo slumped in his chair and shook his head to feign disappointment for the captain to see, but inwardly he was happy. *How could I leave Corsica at a time like this?* The exams had no meaning to him. There was only one thing that existed for him right now—Adrienne.

Besides, there were other things to be taken under serious consideration. Captain Benelli explained why every man was needed. The national situation was going from bad to worse. The war had reached a dizzying speed in North Africa. Even though the Nazi armies under Field Marshal Erwin Rommel relentlessly continued a desperate fight against British Field Marshal Bernard Montgomery's forces, Axis troops were constantly retreating to new positions. Twenty-six divisions—men and officers, including six generals—had abandoned their positions, given up their weapons, and fallen prisoner to the Allied forces. All the presumption of Italian mastery and prestige of desert fighting had been eradicated.

The much-needed sea, which Benito Mussolini proudly called *Mare Nostrum*, was no longer theirs. The navies of Britain and the United States, with their overpowering superiority, had taken sole and permanent possession of it. It was now "their sea."

The troops in Corsica sensed that before long, they too could suffer some kind of assault from the Allied forces, either by air or by sea, and be forced to have a face-to-face confrontation with that mighty power. They all knew that once the mop-up operation in Tunisia was completed, the islands of Sicily, Sardinia, or Corsica would become the logical stepping-stones for the Allies to launch the liberation of Europe.

After Benelli offered this as the rationale for the denial of Renzo's furlough, Renzo said, "It certainly sounds as if there's a strong possibility we will be fighting a battle here in Corsica soon."

But Captain Benelli didn't see it that way. "This retreat in North Africa is just a strategic and temporary pull-back in order to solidify our positions," he reassured Renzo. "And anyway, I have a plan."

"A plan, sir? What plan?"

"Nothing to concern yourself with right now." He dismissed Renzo and then accompanied him out of his office to inspect how well the soldiers had cleaned the yard. Captain Benelli walked throughout the yard, Renzo at his side, and glanced in all directions, searching for any signs of remaining debris. There was a triumphant look in his eyes. Not a shred of paper was seen anywhere. He was pleased by the impact of his own importance, and Renzo could see, clearly written on the captain's brow, that he still nurtured heroic actions.

But there had been something else in his eyes. Renzo could detect the devilish gleam of someone with something up his sleeve.

11 *The Hut*

Although some rain had fallen during the day, a full moon was now shining over the ancient village. The wind that had fiercely howled all day swept away every cloud in the sky, and the stars blinked incessantly. The pleasant scent of eucalyptus and aromatic shrubs rose from the valley, intoxicating Renzo. Adrienne was on his mind.

With each subsequent rendezvous at the grotto, they'd learned more about each other, and their mutual love and respect had grown. Yet each meeting had seemed fresh, and now, as he climbed the hill, looking for the hut—a new location for them—he had the feeling he was seeing her for the first time.

The hut was located well above and to the right of the house, facing the chestnut orchard. At one time it had served as a stable for Monsieur Santi's horses but now, since a new stable had been built before the war broke out, it had become a storage place for hay and other animal feed.

Although old, it still was a sturdy and safe construction. He had no difficulty finding it. The door had been left slightly open and as he entered, his nostrils immediately filled with the pleasant smell of hay bales that were piled up high, way back against a windowless wall. The floor was covered ankle-deep with hay. Nothing else was in the hut except a sturdy, wooden double-manger that had not been used for some time. All was silent inside, and that silence gave Renzo some concern. He feared Adrienne might not be there.

But he quickly saw her. She leaned on the rustic stone wall, gracefully holding her head back and tilted to one side. Her flowing black hair cascaded down her shoulders, covering her back and graciously coming to rest at her slim waist. She stretched her arms toward him as an invitation to come closer, and when he approached, she threw her arms around him and pulled him to her, repeatedly kissing his cheeks, chin, and lips. Renzo held her tightly in his arms, and they stood motionless and silent. Words were not needed; the strong emotions in their hearts were enough. He kissed her cheeks, neck, and warm lips. Resting his head on her heaving breasts for a moment, he gained a sense of calm and then held her hands.

Nothing was studied or rehearsed in his movements. He let go of her hands and knelt in front of her. He instinctively placed his hands on her ankles. Slowly and gently, his fingers found their way up to her knees and thighs, and as they reached her well-rounded hips and crossed to her abdomen, his lips followed the trail his fingers had blazed. He paused for a second, trying to control the flood of blood rushing to his neck and temples. He wished he could have taken command of his impulses, but he couldn't. Unable to hold the tidal wave of hormones at bay, he reached for her silken undergarments and gently pulled them down to the floor.

Adrienne had been silent and still until then, but as Renzo let his hands roam freely over the smoothness of her splendid body, he felt the reaction of muscular tension coming from her quivering flesh, together with a sigh of surrender.

"Please, Renzo, please!" she murmured in a quavering voice, and while firmly holding the lapels of his uniform, she drew him up to again be face-to-face.

One by one he unsnapped the buttons of her polka-dot dress while she, hurriedly and with trembling hands, removed his clothes and piled them with hers on the hay-covered floor.

He kissed her again, and his lips began a journey to the unknown—her lips, chin, neck, and on southward to her perfect breasts and then to her abdomen and thighs. By the time his hands reached her curved hips for a second time, his tongue had already explored the sweetest spot on her magnificent anatomy. There was a gasp, a sigh, and a murmur. Renzo heard his name repeatedly called in a voice no louder than a whisper.

Then slowly, she slithered down from against the wall, almost limp, as if a master puppeteer had let the strings go. They were now both on their knees, facing each other, naked. They fell into another long embrace, and feeling the warmth of her sizzling flesh closely pressed against his, he held her tighter and tighter, as if wanting to fuse their bodies and never to let go again. Their lovemaking was as pure and natural as both had imagined it would be.

A gentle breeze wafted through the open transom, caressing their bodies, while the light of the full moon covered them. They remained quiet for a long time, holding each other in silence, feeling the rhythm of their hearts.

On this island of contrast, on this rock where vendetta and beauty ran parallel, Renzo had found himself. Amid the agony of war and death, he found his life. Except for the sound of a barking dog in the distance, all was silent. Their breathing was scarcely audible. At that moment Renzo couldn't help wondering whether he had just stolen the most valuable and sacred possession a woman has, or if he had just received the most precious gift any man could expect from the woman he loves.

Suddenly, her embrace loosened, and with a sigh, her arms fell to the hay-covered floor; she had lost consciousness. Her brow was covered with cold, clammy perspiration—her breathing somewhat fast and shallow. At first Renzo was concerned, but she was soon breathing slower and more deeply and regained consciousness. He then realized she had never been in danger; she had fainted from exhaustion and exhilaration. Adrienne opened her eyes and saw Renzo's eyes fixed on her.

Pulling him close to her, she whispered, "Thank you, Renzo."

"I love you, Adrienne" is all he could manage to say.

"And I love you," she purred.

Adrienne's eyes reflected a sparkling glow. Renzo leaned in, stared into her eyes, and kissed her deeply.

****

While Renzo and Adrienne were lost in each other's arms, they lost track of time. Even though the moon had disappeared, a brilliant, starlit sky, visible through the transom, kept them from being in the dark. Adrienne snuggled against his chest, giving Renzo the feeling of gaining all the pleasures of life while losing all its pains. They were in the midst of circumstances and events beyond their control. They could only take comfort in having each other.

Although it had been warm and pleasant most of the evening, it had become somewhat damp and cool. Gusts of fresh air filtered into the hut from the open transom, making Adrienne uncomfortable. Renzo wrapped his coat around her, overlapping it around her neck. They looked into each other's eyes and simultaneously burst into long, cheerful laughter.

What a difference in Adrienne since they'd first met. He had been a victim to her standoffish greeting when she opened the door on his first visit to her home and uncaring attitude when he had so clumsily fallen from the staircase. As their relationship developed she'd showed happiness with demure smiles or slight giggles, but this was the first time she had openly laughed with such exuberance. Together, they realized that the uniform she hated so vehemently no longer represented a threat or a symbol of oppression; it was simply a flannel garment, offering warmth and protection.

She had accepted Renzo; accepted his uniform. The sound of her rich laughter gave him an added sense of assurance—the conviction that it hadn't been only their bodies that meshed into one but their spiritual and emotional being as well.

They rose from the hay-covered floor and fell into a playful mood. Renzo placed his cap on her head, and with mock solemnity, he saluted her. "What a beautiful soldier you make!" he said.

"I'm at your command, sir." She responded like an obedient recruit, saluting him in return with the reverence of a soldier to his commanding officer.

"I command you to … accept my love," Renzo said, somewhat awkwardly.

She smiled at his offer and once again fell into his arms. But that burst of genuine joy wasn't long-lasting. A veil of sobriety and sadness descended on her face. "What's going to happen to us now?" she asked.

"We will wait patiently for the war to end."

"And then?"

"Then I will return to Corsica and, with the blessings of your grandparents, we will marry," he reassured her.

"And in the meantime?" she asked.

He had no answer for her. They both knew the risks.

They tried to console each other with the hope that the war would soon be over, and with that in mind, they decided it was time for Renzo to return to La Grande Maison.

He was fully dressed by then—except for his boots. Fearing that the hobnails in his boots would be too noisy on the cobblestone path and attract attention, he decided he would carry them.

It was a long good-bye. Neither could loosen the embrace.

"*Adieu, mon amour*," he said.

"Not *adieu*, but *au revoir*," she corrected him. Weeping, she then asked, "Will you come again tomorrow?"

He nodded. "Yes."

They were in the darkness of predawn when he opened the creaking door and stepped out. He could still get back to La Grande Maison and the infirmary before anyone knew he was missing—anyone except Tonelli, the one person Renzo had trusted with the knowledge of his frequent meetings with Adrienne.

He paused shortly and took a deep, long breath of fresh air. The moon had disappeared, the stars faded, and the glimmering of a pinkish light crossed the horizon and penetrated the sky. A continuous rhythm of heat lightning gave out flashes, making Renzo think of the aurora borealis. He turned around to take a last look at the hut, amazed that they had been able to do something that neither had done before as well as they had.

Furtively, he went down the hill carrying his heavy boots, one in each hand. He was still in a trance-like state when he was brutally forced to come back to earth. A fierce-looking dog jumped out from a narrow alley, breathing heavily, growling madly, and racing toward Renzo. When the dog was at arm's length from him, it came to a sliding stop, with its legs solidly planted on the ground and its mouth dripping with foam.

Renzo had never been in a situation like this—he was face-to-face with a big, unleashed mad dog, at a time when he was supposed to be sleeping in his cot. What would happen if the villagers, who by now may have been rising from their sleep, discovered him? He was unabashedly scared, not so much of the people but of the dog.

If I only knew what would make a dog retreat. Trembling, he felt beads of sweat rolling down his face in rivulets. He didn't have a plan of attack or of defense—only a bizarre thought. What would Napoleon do in such a situation? What did it matter? The Little Corporal wasn't there to give any help. And so, Renzo began to resign himself to the fact that his only salvation was to find a way to outsmart the fierce beast.

He moved slowly, keeping his eyes on the dog, and pasted himself against the wall of the nearest house, a few feet away. He made sure that there was enough room to slide to one side or the other, so that if the dog lunged at him, the animal would crack its head against the wall.

Slowly and carefully, he raised his hands, which were gloved inside the boots, and opened his arms wide, waiting for the dog's decision. It had become a staring confrontation. Renzo didn't know how he appeared to the dog, but he could see its eyes getting redder, shinier, and more intense. With his boots on his hands, he felt safe, as well as somewhat aggressive. An unexpected surge of energy flowed through him. Suddenly, Renzo furiously slammed the boots together, as if he were playing cymbals in a symphony orchestra. The impact was not only crisp and loud, but as the hobnails on the boots crashed together, they sparked brightly, as if they were flashing miniature lightning.

At that sight, the startled dog stood erect on its hind legs, spun around sideways like a recoiling spring, leaped away from Renzo, and quickly ran back to the alleyway, yapping as it disappeared in the darkness. For a brief moment, Renzo felt happy and victorious—and invincible as well.

12 *The Captain's Cannons*

S oon after the strange newspaper-shredding incident, Renzo's
suspicion of Captain Benelli's mental instability became a
certainty.

One morning the captain came down from his quarters and burst
into the infirmary with a seldom-seen attitude. There was a spring in
his step and a gloating gleam in his eyes. Renzo had not yet finished
his breakfast when Benelli requested his backrub. Renzo had known
the captain long enough to know when it was permissible to ask
questions and when it wasn't. And he could see in the way the captain
moved about that this was a time to wait.

Captain Benelli appeared unusually animated and extremely
happy, to the point that he couldn't contain himself. Renzo soon
learned, in minute detail, the reason for the captain's disposition.
Shortly after he began the backrub, Captain Benelli became a font of
information. "Renzo, yesterday I executed a plan I have been thinking
about for quite a while. It will change the course of the war!"

Used to the captain's hyperbole and high opinion of himself,
Renzo simply said, "Wonderful, sir. What have you done, if I may
ask?"

"I took it upon myself. No need to consult with any other
officers."

"Yes, sir. Very bold of you."

"Early in the morning I requisitioned two telegraph poles from
the Corps of Engineers. Then I had some of the men haul two old,
discarded, unusable donkey carts from some abandoned farm and

had everything delivered to the top of the hill that overlooks the west side of the coast. You know, not too far from where the other pieces of light artillery are positioned."

Renzo kept working on the captain's back muscles, feeling the tension slowly dissipate. "Very interesting, sir."

"Oh, there's more. I ordered some men to dismantle the donkey carts, keeping only the skeleton frame, wheels, and sidebars, and had them positioned thirty meters apart. Then they cut the telegraph poles down to the size of heavy artillery, painted them black, and placed them over the axles of the carts—back end on the ground, front end pointing to the sky and aimed at the African coast. Two fake cannons! I had the men throw two large camouflage nets over them to hide the fact that they were shams. To the eyes of the faraway British navy, they might well appear to be the two heaviest caliber cannons on the entire coastline of Corsica!"

"Incredible, sir." Renzo tried his best to hide his amazement that the captain actually believed this was a good plan. "What made you think of it?"

"This is why you're still a private, Crespi. You don't pay attention to modern military tactics."

"Please teach me, then."

"I learned this strategy from General Rommel; not directly, of course, but from hearing about him from other great military leaders. At El Alamein, Rommel strategically positioned dummy wooden tanks, which were mounted on Volkswagens, among the real tanks in order to exaggerate his strength and to intimidate and discourage the British from engaging him in battle." The captain shifted in the massage chair to look a Renzo, as if he wanted his opinion or consent, but he didn't wait for a response. "If it's good enough for the Desert Fox, it's good enough for me. Don't you think?"

It was clear that, at least in his mind, Captain Benelli had achieved his ultimate quixotic dream—to scare the hell out of the English army. Little did he foresee that not long after, on May 13, 1943, the Nazi forces in North Africa would capitulate and surrender to the Allies. The Desert Fox would fall in defeat and be immensely humiliated by British general Bernard Montgomery and American general George Patton.

The captain's revelation of his plans convinced Renzo that his eccentric captain had already crossed the thin line of sanity to the other side.

****

Benelli's injudicious, whimsical act of unilateral decision-making at such a level and his flagrant abuse of authority didn't go unnoticed for long. Word of the captain's wavering stability raced up the chain of command. General Headquarters didn't approve or condone arbitrary actions of this sort—even if they were clever and astute.

The credibility of the Italian prestige and the army's power in Corsica incurred the risk of being undermined and ridiculed. But because of the recognition due to the captain for past achievements, they decided that no admonishment was needed. His judgment, although poor and inappropriate, was not considered a rigid demonstration of the arrogance of power but a symptom of a stress-related emotional disturbance. It was evident that in addition to his delusional behavior, the strain of running a large company proved to be too much for him. It was also obvious that he was no longer able to cope with the mounting pressures of such a task.

As such, an immediate transfer was recommended as not only appropriate but also necessary. It was emphasized, however, that such a transfer was to be considered neither a promotion nor a demotion but an honest effort from General Headquarters to lower the level of the captain's responsibility, thus avoiding the possibility of a complete breakdown and, more important, to restore him back to health.

****

The captain's farewell speech didn't disappoint Renzo. He listened with the rest of the company as Captain Benelli addressed the men with his brief comments.

"Men, I will soon be leaving as your captain. Lieutenant Semprefedele will assume command. He is a good man and a fine leader. I know you will give him the same respect that you afforded me. I am extremely grateful for your dedication during this unique period in our nation's history. There may have been times when my methods seemed harsh or overbearing. Be assured that it was because I know what you men are capable of, and I wanted to bring out the best in you. I believe I accomplished that. You are brave and noble men and are the basis on which Italy will continue to grow and prosper into the greatest nation in Europe, one of the greatest in the world.

"I also felt that because we are living in difficult times, decisions needed to be made on the basis of their ultimate results, not on whether they met with everyone's approval. In due time you will be back home, with your family and friends, and the events here will become memories. Your experiences will follow you into your lives back home, making you the finest leaders in your chosen professions. Maybe some of you will decide to become career military men, like me. I wish you all the best both, here and at home. May God bless you all."

Although a little shorter than his standard speeches, there was no denying his heartfelt emotion. Renzo excused the self-serving portions of the speech, knowing it was an attempt by the captain to maintain his dignity. He felt it was one of the finest speeches he had ever heard from the captain. Even if at times Captain Benelli had been a little overbearing and a little dramatic, it saddened Renzo to see him prepare to depart; he was unsure of whether they would ever see each other again. But he also had a reason to rejoice. The expression on the captain's face showed that he was definitely pleased with his speech. As Renzo hoped, Captain Benelli exploded with a clear, loud, and long sneeze, which was followed by an extended round of applause and raucous cheering from the entire company. In spite of the captain's many idiosyncrasies, the men realized that he was an integral part of their day-to-day lives, and his absence would make life in Corsica that much less interesting and unpredictable.

13 *Lieutenant Semprefedele*

Renzo felt melancholy when he first saw the captain's desk completely cleaned out of all his personal belongings. Gone were the photographs of his dear parents, as was the ibex horn. Only a few surface scratches made by the constant removal and replacing of his cherished trophy remained—not deep scratches but noticeable enough to be a perennial reminder that at one time, Captain Giancarlo Maria Francesco Benelli had been there.

Sadly, Renzo recognized that it was no longer the captain's desk. It was, however, comforting and reassuring to see a worthy officer like Lieutenant Vittorio Semprefedele sitting behind it. No one else had been considered. The company was a large one, and any average or ordinary officer taking charge, especially after the long tenure of Captain Benelli, would have failed.

But Lieutenant Semprefedele was neither average nor ordinary. Unlike Captain Benelli, he was completely approachable; he was a soldier's soldier. He wore a soldier's uniform, not that of an officer. He ate his meals with the soldiers, not at the officers' mess. And he slept on a cot in his office, not in any residential quarters. He was completely unpretentious.

Because he was always scattering breadcrumbs around the grounds to feed the birds, the men affectionately called him Saint Francis of Assisi. In contrast to Captain Benelli, who had been an overbearing and fastidious taskmaster who couldn't stand seeing any soldier idle, Semprefedele was more lenient and more understanding.

He was an extremely well-versed man who never failed to help anyone in need, in any way—physically, financially, or spiritually.

His first official act was the immediate dismantling of the wooden cannons, thus eliminating the need for extra guard duty. Within days, he purchased—with his own money—all the straw and cornhusks needed to replace the hay in the men's sleeping sacks, which had become hard dust. He bought chestnut flour to bake bread as a supplement to their rations, along with some poultry for special occasions. To him, the men were his family and spending his salary for their welfare made him happy.

In addition, he merited their unconditional gratitude due to one distinct action he took on their behalf. It concerned a problem the men had recently experienced—they were assailed by an infestation of head lice.

Renzo distributed all the medication at his disposal in the infirmary, but it was with little success. His appeal to Captain Benelli had gone unheeded. Evidently, the captain had been much too concerned about more important things, to his thinking. But while the captain fought his own demons, the proliferation of those little pests continued. Once Lieutenant Semprefedele took over, he requested immediate help from the field hospital. They promptly sent a truck equipped with a rotating oven, on which their clothes were baked over and over, until victory over the bugs was achieved and the problem solved.

In a short time he had earned the admiration and the respect of not only the company but the entire regiment. He proved to be an officer without equal. Even the civilians showed a certain amount of tolerance for him. They openly greeted him when he walked through the village and actually smiled and shook his hand. In order to reverse the low prestige the company had with the local authorities, he lifted all the restrictions imposed by Captain Benelli. This decision ensured the autonomy of the civilians' political and civil life, as it was elsewhere in Corsica, but still reserved the right for the company to exercise their power to defend themselves from any attempt of an invasion from the Allies.

Church bells rang again. People were allowed to meet, and many activities were restored. Women could say their rosary undisturbed, and men could play their card games or checkers as they wished. Lieutenant Semprefedele never chased children away; he fed them instead. As Semprefedele explained to the vice prefect, "We are here as protectors, not as oppressors."

It was, in a way, as if he had offered the villagers an olive branch that they had accepted, albeit with some reservations. Semprefedele stood firm in denying permission to carry firearms, even for hunting season. The legitimate fear that such weapons could be used against his company lingered on.

14 *Tonelli's Conquest*

Renzo thought he knew all there was to know about Tonelli from Tonelli's own accounts, including his numerous sexual escapades. Renzo knew of the superficiality of Tonelli's actions as well as the occasional depth of his thinking. He knew Tonelli's shortcomings as well as his strong points. Tonelli was as vain a person as Renzo had ever met, but he was also a faithful friend. There was no one else Renzo could have trusted with his secrets. But as time went by, Renzo discovered there was more to learn about him.

One night as Renzo entered the infirmary following a rendezvous with Adrienne, he saw Tonelli dancing alone in front of a mirror, bowing and curtsying as he softly hummed the tune of a Mozart minuet. He knew that Tonelli was one of those narcissists who, when passing a mirror, could never resist stopping to take a peek. But this was not a simple glimpse. Hat in hand, he stood there, blowing kisses to an imaginary damsel, and softly talking to the mirror—not to give compliments to a phantom lady but to tell her that he was the greatest.

When he saw Renzo standing silently by the door, he bowed his head in Renzo's direction in mock gallantry and smiled widely. This odd behavior in the middle of the night aroused Renzo's curiosity and made him wonder what Tonelli was up to. Something was different about him. For one thing, Renzo noticed that the usual neatness of his uniform was gone. His hair was rumpled and his necktie askew. The tips of his shoes, as well as his elbows and the knees of his pants, were wet and stained, as if he had been crawling on the grassy ground.

"What's going on here?" Renzo asked casually, thinking that perhaps Tonelli might be drunk.

Without hesitation and with much pomp, Tonelli answered, "Renzo, congratulations are in order. My army-imposed celibacy has finally come to an end."

"Meaning what?"

"Now I can proudly say that I am an international lover," he declared with his usual braggadocio.

"What are you talking about?" Renzo asked.

Tonelli approached him as if he was about to reveal a big military secret. "I've just had a bite of the most tender meat in all of Corsica."

"What kind of game are you playing? Is this a ridiculous riddle?"

"No, it's neither a game nor a riddle. But I'll be more specific." Tonelli came closer, and with his lips almost grazing Renzo's ear, he said in a staccato voice, "I have just made love to the most provocative and cooperative girl on the island."

"It must have been one hell of a dream!" Renzo teased.

"No, no, no. This is no dream. Let me tell you!" Without stopping to catch his breath, he continued. "Magnificent breasts, silky white skin. And she tastes as sweet as honey."

"When and where did you meet this supposed vixen?" Renzo asked, still incredulous.

"While you've been busy with your own angel, I had one of my own."

"You never mentioned anything to me."

"I didn't realize I needed to keep you informed of all my activities."

"So you roamed the village, looking for women, while I've been away?"

"You are forgetting—I am Alvaro Tonelli," he said, proudly. "I didn't have to go looking anywhere for her. She came to me!" His vanity and ego knew no bounds.

"And who might this girl be?" Renzo asked.

"It's someone you know. I've seen her with you many times."

"With me?"

"Yes. Corinne."

The mention of Corinne's name struck Renzo like a thunderbolt. His initial reaction was one of surprise and amazement, but then a feeling of uneasiness came over him. He knew Corinne well and could not conceive, believe, or accept that the admission could be true. Corinne was the girl who lived next door to La Grande Maison. She was the mayor's daughter. Renzo couldn't imagine her becoming Tonelli's newest conquest.

Corinne might have appeared to be a little bit of a flirt, but Renzo always attributed her demeanor to her bubbly and friendly personality. He had never seen her without a cheek-to-cheek rosy smile. She had never failed to stop Renzo and start a conversation about many little things. She had come to him often, either to offer him little bunches of wildflowers she had freshly picked or to give him some local delicacies, such as *fiadone*, a type of cheesecake, or a link of wild-boar sausage, which he always accepted with pleasure.

Occasionally, she would demurely approach Renzo, seeking his help to fix her old, dilapidated bicycle, on which she would usually come speeding down the road, wearing a scruffy dress, her long hair flying in the wind. Or she would pass La Grande Maison, prancing and swishing her hips and tossing her head from side to side, skipping a knotted, frayed rope and leaving behind clouds of dust, while her prematurely developed bosom bounced and swayed seductively beneath her multicolored sweater.

She was very attractive and somewhat sensuous to look at, but Renzo couldn't imagine having any sensual thoughts about her. He just couldn't conceive how anyone in his right mind would ever nourish any sexual ambitions for her. For one thing, she had a certain aura of innocence that served as a shield.

Also, Corinne was only fourteen years old.

"What kind of animal are you, anyway?" Renzo exploded in disgust. "I've always respected you, in spite of some of your flaws, but you have disappointed me, my friend. Imagine that! Taking advantage of a young girl that age! You should be ashamed of yourself."

"I couldn't help it. I gave in to temptation. I surrendered to her lure. She seduced me!" he said, as if he were the victim.

"She seduced *you*? An immature, naïve, fourteen-year-old schoolgirl has seduced you, a sophisticated man of the world? How can that happen?"

There was no quick answer. But a few seconds later, still unruffled, Tonelli began to recount how things had happened. "Well, let me tell you. One evening about a month ago, while I was playing my guitar at the foot of the dividing wall between La Grande Maison and the mayor's house, she started a conversation with me from the other side of the wall. Keep in mind that she started speaking to me. She told me how much she enjoyed my music and how lovely and romantic it would be if I would serenade her sometime.

"So tonight, that 'sometime' arrived. We were again on opposite sides of the wall and made some small talk for a while. She told me about some French novels she had read and described some of the sexier parts in great detail. I've been learning some Corsican folk songs, and when she asked me to play, I dedicated one to her. Apparently, the books inspired her and taught her a few things. She became so aroused by the books and my music that she encouraged me to jump over the wall, where, right there on the ground, my charms and her unrestrained desires met."

"That's preposterous!" Renzo said. "Making love to a child."

"Listen, Renzo. When a fisherman goes to sea, he doesn't ask the fish he catches how old it is. He's only interested in its size. The same goes for the hunter. He doesn't ask the pheasant he is hunting for a birth certificate. All he wants to know is how much meat there is under that mass of feathers. Right? Well, do you have any idea what's under that untidy dress? I assure you, it's not a child's body!"

His flippant analogy stunned Renzo. For a moment, he couldn't say a word, but then he finally managed to speak. "You've got to stop this nonsense. It's indecent, and it's immoral."

"Is it?" Tonelli asked with a touch of sarcasm.

"Yes. It's intolerable. Remember, she's only fourteen. Do you understand the consequences this would bring if it were discovered? For one thing, she has two brothers—Pierre and Marcel—and if they find out, they'll kill you!"

"How are they going to find out? She has sworn to secrecy, and I certainly won't tell."

"I also must remind you that headquarters would never condone this dishonorable act, especially when it involves an underage girl. You could be severely disciplined, perhaps even court-martialed."

"I'll take my chances," Tonelli said curtly. "And besides, my puritan friend, aren't you doing the same thing you're condemning me for?"

"In some respects, but there are important differences. First of all, Adrienne is an adult, and secondly, we love each other," Renzo stated firmly. "I doubt that love is a part of your shameful behavior."

"Of course I love her!" Tonelli snapped. "I love her inviting, sexy lips. I love her big, smooth breasts. And I love her firm, round ass."

"That's lust, not love," Renzo insisted. "Love is more than a few minutes of physical pleasure. You've completely obscured the meaning of love."

"Oh, well, Renzo, to each his own. *Vive le difference!*" Tonelli concluded as he undressed for bed.

It was late, and Renzo knew that all his exhortations had gone nowhere. As much as he tried to dissuade Tonelli from continuing his obscene madness, he knew it was a futile effort. In addition, he didn't want to engage in any personal confrontation—they needed each other. Tonelli had offered to lie to their officers and give excuses for Renzo if his absence was noticed, and Renzo sensed that, from now on, Tonelli would need Renzo's help in return.

Paying no attention to Renzo, Tonelli adroitly eluded the guards on duty, from then on and every night. With the agility of a panther and the appetite of a hyena he continued to jump over the wall and make passionate love to his wild-eyed Corinne. And she, with open arms—docile as a kitten and submissive as a slave—would faithfully wait alongside the blooming rosebush and fall into the arms of Renzo's immoral and salacious friend, who never regretted his actions and never was found out. Out of necessity and self-preservation, Tonelli, Corinne, and Renzo kept the secret. Tonelli's actions were so contrary to Renzo's morals that he decided he wouldn't even tell Adrienne.

15 *News from Adrienne*

June was not a good month for the company. Ever since the victory of the Allies over the Germans, when Generals Patton and Montgomery brought the Desert Fox to his knees, a mantle of nervousness covered everyone. With the fall of Tunisia, where approximately 275,000 German and Italian troops were taken prisoner, the African campaign ended. The shame of such a terrible defeat was devastating to their morale.

Although the optimism of youth and the continuous speeches of their superiors had them still believing in their survival, no one was convinced there was any chance to win the war. It wasn't a matter of *if* but of *when* the end would come. They were fully aware that as soon as the mop-up operation in North Africa was over, the Allies would resume their unstoppable march for the liberation of Europe.

They felt sure, however, that the Allies' future objective wouldn't be Corsica. They were convinced that their first stepping-stone would be either Sicily or Sardinia, which were logical first steps for Allied forces coming from North Africa.

Strangely, however, it was not the British or American armies that they feared; it was fear of insurrection by the Maquisards. In the previous few months the Maquisards had received a large amount of weapons on the southwest coast of Corsica, coming from Algeria on the French submarine *Casablanca* and from nightly parachute drops from American and British planes. Not every delivery was successful, however. There were many instances when, due to the vigilant observance of the Coast Guard, the Italian army had been able to confiscate sizeable quantities of weapons and made many arrests of the plotting Maquisards. Soon after, because of the Italians' intensified watch in the region and because of the Allies' failed attempts, the submarine deliveries were halted for a while and the aerial drop site changed.

Rumors circulated among the troops that with all probability, the Maquisards would choose their region. There was no basis in fact or any particular information to substantiate these rumors. They were simply based on a growing fear that existed because of a lack of positive news. As a result, life in the company was forever changed. The possibility of a surreptitious attack from an unseen and unknown assailant—the partisans—had their nerves frazzled and rubbed raw. Everybody became suspect. Anyone seen after sunset was stopped, searched, and interrogated for possible cooperation to conspiracy. Some of Captain Benelli's orders, originally thought to be bordering on paranoia, were reinstated. The church bells ceased to chime, and all gatherings of groups larger than three needed to be approved by Lieutenant Semprefedele, under the threat of military arrest. With the current concerns, the company was forced to alter their stagnant military routine. Security had been tightened and, except for the night patrol, no one was allowed to leave his post.

For Renzo, his fear was overcome by his love for Adrienne, although under the circumstances their meetings became impossible. All they had to comfort them was the memory of the time they had spent together.

****

The first week of July was a week of unbearable, scorching heat, and this day seemed to be the worst of them all. The sirocco wind had slowly come up from the coast of Africa, and the air grew heavy and intolerable. It was a day of such high temperature that the troops could feel their strength slowly seeping out of their bodies, discouraging any activity. But Renzo longed to see Adrienne. When night fell and the air cooled off a bit, he ventured to climb the hill, defying all ordinances and hoping that Adrienne would be there. She was.

And as he entered the hut, she came to him hurriedly and fell into his arms with the same warmth and passion as ever. Yet a strange feeling in her embrace instantly suggested to Renzo that something troubled her. The way she hugged him, the way she lay her head on his chest, the way she never loosened her trembling arms gave him reason for alarm. It was the kind of embrace that seemed to beg for understanding and compassion.

Renzo gently held her face in the palms of his hands and tenderly lifted her head away from his chest to take a closer look at her. Although only a dim light filtered into the hut from the transom, he could see an absent, worried, unhappy stare, with an opaqueness he never had seen in her eyes. A mask of tension covered her face. For a short time it was eerily quiet in the hut.

Renzo, trying to lift her spirits, broke the silence. "Did you miss me that much?" he asked.

She nodded.

"I missed you, too. I've wanted to come up many times, but there are problems that I needed to deal with. Did you think I wasn't going to come up anymore?"

She shook her head. "I've come here every day, hoping to see you."

"Why the tears, then? I'm here now!"

She didn't speak but tightened her arms around him, sobbing.

"What is it? What's disturbing you so much?"

She hesitated and then, with tears in her eyes and a trembling voice, said, "I'm pregnant. Two months along."

Renzo's initial reaction, fueled by his naiveté and love of Adrienne, was one of elation. The political and cultural reality that surrounded him didn't enter his thoughts. Looking in her eyes, however, he noticed with sadness that there was too much terror in them.

"Does this please you?" she asked, looking disappointed. The trembling tone in her voice stopped him from expressing his immense happiness, but he had to answer.

"Of course. This is wonderful news."

"No, it isn't. I can't go through with it. I won't go through with it," she said firmly.

"Why not? This will strengthen our love."

"No. This will divide us, maybe forever."

"Why?"

Adrienne paused briefly, gathering her thoughts. She held Renzo's hand tightly and led him to the wooden manger for her to lean on. "Please listen to me," she began. "For one thing, this pregnancy is not just proof of an indiscretion but a badge of shame as well. Once discovered, I will be accused of being a fornicator and the village harlot. And worse, the child will have no name. He will be known as the illegitimate fruit of a clandestine love. A bastard! That's what he will be called. The villagers will surely pin a label on him that will become an emblem of disgrace, which will live forever. And because you are an enemy, they would consider his birth my national betrayal. Is that what you want, Renzo? And how could I ever face my grandpapa, the stern moralist that he is?"

She paused to wipe her tear-filled eyes. "You see, to us Corsicans, there is no treasure more valuable than honor. Nothing! No riches, no gold, no silver, no possessions. Honor is sacred to us. And being the last member of our family, I surely can't be the one to bring shame and dishonor to seven generations of a proud family, one of the most highly esteemed families in all of Corsica. And now, because of me, their spotless reputation will be stained forever. And what about Grandmama? She would rather die than live in disgrace. She couldn't endure it, and I don't want her to be ridiculed by society for my shameful indiscretions."

Now she was weeping profusely. Renzo held her in his arms and she continued. "Do you have any idea what the partisans are doing to women who have committed acts of collaboration with the occupying forces, especially if those acts are of a sexual nature? They bring them to the public square and shave their heads as the entire population watches. And that's not all. After that vilifying ordeal, they force them to walk home naked, wearing only their shoes. I've seen this recently in a nearby village, where two women were submitted to such an atrocious and inhuman punishment." She now sounded harsh. Her voice no longer had that lilt that he loved so much, and as she spoke, the visual image of her going through such a humiliation made his legs and arms stiffen with horror. That sad, detailed explanation of her legitimate fears broke his heart. "Do you understand now, Renzo? I just can't go through with it," she said emphatically.

"What is the alternative?"

"I will abort," she simply said.

"How could you even think of that? It would be an unforgivable abomination. You would bring the wrath of God upon yourself and your family."

"Haven't we already incurred God's wrath by doing what we have been doing all the while? Aren't you aware of that?"

"Yes, I am, but one sin in God's eye shouldn't justify another. And we should not let the fear of what others think or do influence us. We must search within ourselves to find the right solution. One thing I know: it's wrong to commit abortion. You may look for the rest of your life for a greater joy than giving birth, but you'll never find it. You wouldn't be able to live with yourself. This will haunt you forever, not just because you've snuffed a life but because the life you have snuffed was part of us."

She listened attentively, but not a muscle in her face ever moved. Hoping to influence her, he pleaded with her in the name of love.

"Our love will overcome this," he said. "We must have faith. If this is our destiny, let it be. We can neither escape it nor fight it." She stared past him, silent, her eyes misting. Renzo continued. "If the war goes on at this pace it won't be long before it's over, and all our fears will be forgotten."

"Do you really believe that?" She forced a slight smile. "The war will be over soon, and we could begin a life together?"

"I do. Everything I've heard recently would indicate that."

"What have you heard?"

"Nothing official, of course, but the troops believe that the Allied power is too overwhelming for Germany. If they can't sustain the war effort, neither will we."

Those words seemed to have a reassuring effect on her. She lifted her head as if a great weight had been removed from it. Her smile widened, brightening her face, and she gave Renzo a reassuring nod. "You are right," she said.

His words touched her deeply, and he was moved at her willingness to relent. But one question still remained on Renzo's mind.

"Where and how would you have gone for the abortion? There are no means of transportation and no doctors in the village."

"Domenica knows a woman nearby who is capable, safe, and very secretive."

That name shook him up. He was astounded. "Domenica? Your housemaid knows about this?"

Adrienne nodded and answered almost matter-of-factly. "Yes, Domenica knows everything about us. In fact, she had predicted that we were destined to fall in love with each other the very moment you stepped into our house for dinner, and she knew all along that something like this would happen."

"Do you trust Domenica enough to confide all our secrets to her?"

"I would entrust her with my life!"

"Was it she who prompted you to this foolish decision?"

"No. She is also against it. She was only obeying my wish."

That assertion calmed Renzo's spirit as well. To know that the old housekeeper, the woman who had taken care of Adrienne since her birth, shared his opinion made him feel as if he had gained an ally. He was now positive that Adrienne wouldn't change her mind again and go through with such a decision.

"I've been away too long. I should get back to La Grande Maison." Renzo gave Adrienne a long, tight embrace and a deep kiss. Renzo left the hut with a grateful heart, and as he was pulling the door shut behind him, he turned to ask, "Is there anything I can do?"

She looked at him with a smile and affectionately rumpled his hair with a brisk rub of her hand. She shook her head. "No, no, no," she said. "You've done enough already!"

16 *Invasion of Sicily*

Negative news reports during the last weeks of July caused a downward spiral of such intensity that the company found it impossible to maintain any hope for the future. They didn't have to be genius military strategists to objectively evaluate the seriousness of the situation. It was clear that before long, the Allies would spread out far and wide until they reached Corsica. One by one the smaller islands in the Mediterranean Sea fell to the British and American armies. First came Pantelleria and Lampedusa as appetizers, and they anticipated that Corsica would be the main course. And so, with much concern, a lot of trepidation, and a dash of fear, they waited.

Security tightened. The gasoline depot, and food and water supplies were all kept under strict watch. But Corsica was not yet on the Allies' agenda; Sicily was. On July 10, General Montgomery's British Eighth Army, General Patton's American Seventh Army, and a powerful Anglo-American naval force landed on the sandy coast of the southernmost province of Sicily.

Rumors spread that no Italian troops participated in the opposition to the Allies. They had supposedly lost the will to fight under German orders or alongside them. Most Italian soldiers quickly exchanged their uniforms for civilian clothes and managed to blend in among the civilians. The less fortunate were taken prisoner by the Allied forces. The only opposition the Allies encountered came from the Germans, who had taken absolute command of Sicily and fought desperately to repel any attack. It was all in vain. Within a week the

Anglo-American forces steadily and decisively forced the Germans to retreat. Not long after, on July 22, they captured Palermo, the capital, liberating Sicily from the retreating Nazis.

The company followed the events with great interest, but war news suddenly took secondary place to a more significant bulletin coming from Rome. On July 24, to the sorrow of some, the delight of many, and the surprise of all, the now-sickly Benito Mussolini, the once powerful and bellicose Il Duce, was forced by the Great Council of the Ministers to submit his resignation. His removal from power ended twenty years of strong-armed dictatorship. King Vittorio Emanuele III had him arrested and confined at Campo Imperatore on Mount Gran Sasso in the Abruzzi region. Mussolini left behind a legacy of enormous disappointments. Not only had all the promises he made to his people remained a visionary's dream, but also he miserably failed to fulfill his own ambition to restore Italy to the glory of the old Roman Empire. Even worse, he had sacrificed Italy and its initiative by wrapping it in a mixture of flattery and delusion and promptly offering it up to Hitler.

The decision for Mussolini's replacement was immediate. The king speedily ordered Marshal Pietro Badoglio, a lifelong opponent of the Fascist regime and an old hero of the First World War, to form a new government. He was now the commander in chief of all the Italian armed forces.

That announcement created an uncomfortable period in the already nervous and precarious situation at La Grande Maison. There was a possibility the news would create havoc among the troops, and no one, including the high-ranking officers, knew how to prevent it.

Renzo, Tonelli, and Nino were discussing the latest developments as they took a quick cigarette break from their duties. They sat at the base of the large chestnut tree in the center of the yard.

"What do you think will happen now?" Nino asked.

"Mussolini's shrewd. Maybe Badoglio's in charge, but I don't see Il Duce going quietly," Tonelli responded.

"What do you mean?" Renzo asked. "If he's out, he's out."

"Don't be so sure. You know there are eighty-five thousand Italian forces here, including eight battalions of Fascist militia. So about one-tenth of our troops have strong partisan sentiments for

Mussolini. That may not sound like much, but who can predict what their reaction to this news will be?"

General Magli, commander in chief of all the Italian forces in Corsica, wasted no time. He immediately requested a meeting with the Council General of the militia and the commanders of the various battalions and legions, asking them to define their positions—whether they intended to stay faithful to their oath to the deposed Duce or to continue being integral units of the Italian army.

Their answer was firm, decisive, and encouraging. They made it clear that the black color of their shirts no longer had any meaning. What mattered now was the tricolor—the red, white, and green of Italy. They would no longer fight for Benito Mussolini but for the king. They would no longer march for the ideology of Fascism but for the restoration of their country.

These statements pleased and relieved General Magli. Immediately after that amicable meeting, in order to demonstrate to the population that there was unity among the troops, General Magli issued a bulletin to all the troops in Corsica, urging them to exercise restraint—to not manifest any emotions, whether of joy or sadness, but to be an example of absolute composure—and concluding with "Italians are Italians."

As August approached, with the way the war was going in the Mediterranean, the quietness on the island was quickly disappearing and was replaced by a state of fermenting nervousness. It seemed that the fall of Mussolini had fanned the hatred the Maquisards had for the Italian troops all along. Bandit activity sprouted in many areas. There were several attacks on various Italian military officers and *carabinieri*, with only a few perpetrators brought to justice.

Fortunately, General Magli was not a vindictive man. He didn't allow these acts of the partisans to affect his treatment of the overall population. In fact, in spite of those incidents he demonstrated his strong compassion. A German warship sunk a French cargo ship that was transporting supplies from France to Corsica at a time when the island was suffering through a severe shortage of food. He voluntarily donated approximately 130 tons of flour to be distributed among the neediest Corsican families. The Prefect de la Corse, as well as the population at large, acknowledged this generous act openly and with much gratitude. However, some Maquisards shamelessly continued their acts of sabotage wherever and whenever they could.

Despite these sporadic skirmishes, the company remained focused on the eerie prospect of having weapons dropped in their area. It was obvious that the success of such a mission would imbue the partisans and their leaders with greater passion and more eagerness to fight them. But the partisans were essentially an unidentified force with unknown leadership that the company would have to deal with, making the task that much more treacherous and uncertain.

To add to the dilemma, many of the men rationalized that if it were true that the Italian troops had refused to fight the Allies to protect Sicily, their own land, why should they risk their lives fighting anyone to protect Corsica, a land that wasn't even theirs?

At the same time, the Italian Secret Service continued the intensive hunt for the leader of the partisans to arrest him. Many people were interrogated but with no positive results. Instead, all they found out was that the Corsicans knew how to keep a secret.

The only thing they could do was wait.

17 *Voices*

Renzo was able to see Adrienne more frequently, now that some of the restrictions were eased. But with all the activity at La Grande Maison, things were so uncertain and charged with such anxiety that they could only count on living from day to day.

They were in the hut, quietly lying together with their arms around each other. Through the transom they could occasionally see some small clouds drift lazily across the crescent moon, which enveloped them in complete darkness. The tender moment was broken when strange noises startled them both. Renzo quickly cupped his hand over Adrienne's mouth, and they continued listening to what seemed to be muffled voices, accompanied by the sound of footsteps crunching the tall, dried-up weeds as they neared the hut. The sound came from the people who eventually stopped by the hut, directly next to a half-opened window. Renzo and Adrienne sprang up and carefully leaned against the wall. They heard two distinctly different voices speaking.

"At last, everything is c-c-coming together," said one.

"Yes, we are counting on you to notify everyone that on the night of the twentieth of September, it will rain," said the other.

"Of c-c-course," the first man said with a slight laugh. "The drop. It will rain g-g-guns and ammunition on the open f-f-field between the v-v-vineyard and the chestnut orchard."

The brief conversation led Renzo to believe the men must have been returning from a secret Maquisards meeting in a house not far away.

The speech pattern of the first voice, although somewhat muted, intrigued Renzo. He knew he had heard it before, but he needed to search his memory for where or when. He waited to hear more, but there was no longer any need. Although it had been some time since he'd heard that voice, it suddenly registered in his head. He knew only one man who spoke that way—the stuttering, myopic mayor of the village. Renzo had no trouble identifying the second voice at all. It belonged to Monsieur Santi.

At that moment, a long-lasting shiver shot down his spine. It was the same shiver that he'd felt when Monsieur Santi shook his hand to welcome him into his house, the same shiver that taunted him all through the dinner, the same shiver he'd felt when he shook his hand on the way out of his house—except for one thing: those had been shivers of premonition; this was one of affirmation. The night Renzo met Santi for the first time, he sensed that this was a man to contend with, but he hadn't realized to what extent.

The two men continued to speak, but Renzo no longer heard what they were saying. He trembled with horror. The man who had offered him hospitality and friendship, who had shared his bread and wine with him; the man who had toasted to Renzo's honor, to his family, and to his country; and more important, the man who was the grandfather of the woman he had fallen in love with was one of the leaders of the Maquisards from that sector. Suddenly, an avalanche of negative thoughts assaulted him, along with a chilling fury that shredded his heart. He stiffened up, frozen in anger.

Renzo looked at Adrienne, whose own hands now were cupped over her mouth. Her eyes were wide in astonishment. He wasn't sure whether she was shocked to hear her grandfather's voice, which identified him as a local partisan leader, or if she was ashamed that Renzo now knew what she had been hiding. He wanted to believe the former, but doubts entered his mind. Could it be possible that she'd known all along? Was she as good an actress as she was a pianist? For a while they remained against the wall surrounded by silence until the footsteps moved away into the night, but his heart was racing with doubt and confusion. Their eyes met, and Renzo gave her an assessing, scrutinizing look. He could hardly speak but somehow managed to voice the feelings that were tearing at him. "How much do you know about this?" he asked.

"Nothing, nothing at all," she said. "I am just as surprised as you are."

"Are you?" he asked in a hesitant, sarcastic laugh.

"Of course I am," she said. "Why? Do you suspect me of something?"

"How can I not suspect you? He's your grandfather; you live in the same house; you know all his moves and activities. How can you not know?"

"We each have our own life. He has his affairs to tend to, and I have my books and my music."

Renzo stared at her coldly. "Isn't there anything you share with him, like being a partisan?"

"Oh, Renzo, please don't accuse me of anything. Don't be so blind. You know that I love you. I swear I don't know anything about this. Believe me."

Renzo wanted to believe her but couldn't, even though she sounded somewhat convincing. He had already stopped listening to her. He didn't want to listen. There was no way she couldn't be aware of her grandfather's activities. "You're an accomplice to your grandfather," he accused.

She looked at him, stupefied, as if she were seeing him for the first time. She attempted to shake him out of his obstinate meanness and as she did, tears began to flow freely. "Please, Renzo, don't judge me unjustly. I know nothing of this. Whatever you think of me, remember this—I love you."

He paid no attention to her. He was too deaf to hear and too crazed to listen. "What do you intend to do with all the weapons you are to receive? Kill us all?" he asked with much contempt.

In an uncontrollable impulse, he drew his gun from the bandolier, removed the safety latch from it, and tried to hand it to her. But she stepped aside and put her trembling arms behind her back, refusing to accept it. For a moment Renzo forgot all the kisses, embraces, and lovemaking of the past. All he could see was an enemy standing before him for a final confrontation.

"I thought you had given me a new life, but all I can expect from you now is death," he said. "Here, take the gun. All you have to do is pull the trigger and it will be over. You'll have one less to kill later."

She was still close to him. She embraced him, but his arms remained limp.

"Believe me, *mon amour*, believe me!" she managed to say in a shaky voice. A deathly paleness blanketed her face; her eyes fixed on him in a glazed stare. "Trust me, Renzo. How could you ever suspect that I could do such a thing? I don't want to lose you. I would have no reason to live without you."

Sobbing uncontrollably, she hung on to his arms and slowly slid down, hugging him tightly until her knees reached the hay-covered dirt floor. She repeatedly called his name and kissed his thighs, knees, and feet. But Renzo remained unmoved. His doubts and suspicions had already taken root in his confused head. It was not until she reached up to grasp his hands and brought them to her eyes so that he could feel the warmth of her tears that he realized he had become an impassive, cold, and incredulous being. He'd always trusted people, but slowly, he realized that his outrage had embittered him so much that he'd lost all power of judgment. At that moment, he questioned if Captain Benelli's paranoia could have rubbed off on him. They had been so close for so long that he thought it was a possibility.

"Please, Renzo," Adrienne pleaded. "You must believe me. I never knew anything about Grandpapa's underground activities. I swear to God."

"I need more than that!" he replied, still unable to dispel his doubts.

He thought he knew all there was to know about her, but he didn't know how deep her love for God was, and that rendered her oath meaningless. However, he did know how much love and veneration she nourished for the memory of her deceased parents. Renzo placed the gun back in the bandolier. He grabbed her by the wrist and, not fearing whether they would be seen by anyone, pulled her outside and headed for the family gravesite where her parents were buried. It was a simple tomb, built at the foot of a massive granite boulder on which their names had been chiseled. Adrienne had taken him there before, asking their blessing of her relationship with Renzo. He knew she couldn't lie to them, and once they reached the grave, he forced her to kneel down.

"Here," he said in a severe, challenging tone. "Swear your innocence in front of them. Only then will I believe you!"

She looked at him with pity, and slowly she knelt and repeatedly kissed the cold granite stone, whispering, "Oh, *mon père, ma mère*, make him believe me." Once again she looked at him, tears cascading down her pale cheeks. "Why do you torment me? What else can I do to prove to you that I am innocent? What more can I give you, other than my own life?"

The sincerity of those words left Renzo visibly shaken. He gently reached for her wrist, trying to lift her up, but instead, with her hand as cold as her parents' grave, she pulled him down to his knees alongside her.

She remained silent, but he could see her lips quiver with emotion. Her moving plea had pierced his heart. It took him a while to clear his mind from the emotional fuzziness and to find an objective evaluation of their predicament. But finally, after a long, agonizing inner torment, he looked at the roaming, faraway clouds and angrily pounded his fists to the ground. He burst out in pain, cursing the war and the damage it was inflicting on him and Adrienne.

Slowly, they got to their feet and returned to the hut in silence. Renzo wanted to say something to her, but no words came out. He wanted her to know how sorry he was. He wanted to express his regrets for his accusations. He wanted to make amends for his insane behavior. He wanted to beg her forgiveness, but she put her finger on his lips, her eyes pleading that he say nothing.

That quiet, gentle contact brought him back to sanity. How could he ever have been so harsh, so cruel, and so intransigent? How could she ever condone his senseless and blind anger or for his being the source of so much sorrow and grief? It had been such a horrible nightmare. His heart filled with regret and remorse, and on seeing that sincere expression of innocence in her eyes, he felt even guiltier.

"Could you ever forgive me, *mon amour*?" he asked.

She gave him no answer but threw herself into his arms.

"Renzo," she said, "whatever you think of me, remember one thing: I love you, and I shall die loving you."

"And I will love you forever."

But how long would forever be for them? What had just occurred created a new and graver dilemma. Renzo found himself in the fork of a road, and no matter which side he took, he would be the loser. If he denounced Monsieur Santi, as he knew he should, he could become a hero for having discovered the identity of the local Maquisards leader, something that neither the secret service nor the counter-espionage units had been able to do in many weeks. But by disclosing this, he would be compelled to reveal how, where, and when he had discovered it. This would mean the confession of his blatant disregard of the order not to socialize with the civilians, making him subject to punishment by the military tribunal. Also, if Monsieur Santi were to be arrested and found guilty, Adrienne would lose her grandfather. The partisans would incriminate her for collaborating with an Italian soldier, and she'd be dishonored by having her head shaved in the public square. And Renzo would lose her forever. Last—but most important—was the fact that if he said nothing and it were discovered that he knew about Monsieur Santi, he would be accused of being a traitor to his country, losing not only his honor but Adrienne as well.

There were no good options out of Renzo's awful predicament, and he prayed for a miracle to see him through it.

18 *About-Face*

Renzo had no one to turn to for advice. This seemingly insurmountable problem was his to face alone. For days he performed his duties in a hazy torpor. His demeanor returned to the way it was when he was on his quest to find the girl in the pale blue dress. The matter was too explosive, and Renzo was sure that anyone else—Tonelli, Nino, certainly any officer—would advise him to uncover Monsieur Santi and the mayor as leaders of the local partisan movement.

Renzo knew from the start what he needed to do. He thought of every excuse to avoid it, but ultimately, he faced reality. If Adrienne truly loved him as he loved her, she would understand—or at least find it in her heart to forgive him in time. They would be able to mend their relationship. After all, she showed how deeply she felt about her country when they first met. It would only be natural that Renzo felt the same about his own country and would do what needed to be done to protect Italy. There was too much at stake.

He decided he would go to Lieutenant Semprefedele the next day. He repeatedly rehearsed the story he would tell. Adrienne would be left out of it entirely to protect her from any dishonor. He would say he took a walk and ducked into the hut when he heard Monsieur Santi and the mayor approaching. Renzo might face disciplinary action for leaving his post, but he was prepared to accept it. He didn't know how he and Adrienne would deal with the pregnancy, but there was time to figure that out.

Renzo was unable to sleep. When morning came and he dressed, his hands fumbled as he buttoned his shirt. Lieutenant Semprefedele was a good man, Renzo reasoned. He would be lenient with any punishment.

As Renzo walked through the yard, he saw the lieutenant briskly walking in his direction. Renzo stood at attention and saluted. "Sir, I need to speak with you on an important matter."

Semprefedele returned the salute. "Not now, Renzo. I need to discuss something with the other officers. There have been some major developments. I'll call for you when I have time."

The lieutenant continued on his way. He never called for Renzo—the request to speak with the lieutenant was forgotten in the excitement of the day's events.

As Renzo soon discovered, an event of historic proportions made his dilemma disappear. Monsieur Santi's prediction of the potential mid-September "rain" never came to pass. There was no longer any reason for it. That day, September 8, 1943, Lieutenant Semprefedele received a message from General Magli, stating that emissaries representing Italy's new prime minister, Marshal Pietro Badoglio, and America's General Dwight D. Eisenhower had signed an armistice on September 3 between all Italian armed forces and the American, British, and French powers.

Renzo, Tonelli, and Nino joined the rest of the company in greeting the news with a chaotic uproar, a mixture of joy and sadness—joy because they believed the armistice meant cessation of firing on anyone and not being fired upon, and sadness because it also meant the certainty that they had lost the war.

The news of the armistice quickly swept through the village. The women piously rushed to church, repeatedly making the sign of the cross and thanking the Virgin Mary, giving her credit for having performed a miracle in the signing of the armistice—September 8 is the feast of the Virgin Mary in Corsica—ignoring the fact that it was actually signed on September 3. The men, offering bread, cheese, and wine, came to meet the Italian troops. They made their first tentative steps to acknowledge the change in status of their former enemies.

Although they didn't yet know or imagine what else was in store for them, the surprised troops made an attempt to hide their ingrained suspicions of the villagers and gladly accepted their initiative. From that moment on, things began to move rapidly. Before sunset, General Magli requested a meeting with General Fridolin von Senger, commander of the German forces in Corsica. It was a short, cold meeting in which the Italian armistice was discussed. At one point General von Senger asked General Magli for his assistance and his support in the event of a German evacuation to Italy—specifically, the use of Italian transport ships anchored in the port of Bastia, plus some Italian transport planes on the airbase of Borgo. The response of General Magli was negative. "There's nothing we can do for you, General. We might consent not to interfere with your using the roads to Bastia, but we can no longer get militarily involved. You, yourselves, are responsible for your own safety. Our war is over!"

The indignant German general was appalled at such a staunch refusal. Until then, the Germans had been the dominant force in the alliance with Italy, but now that the Axis no longer existed, he felt his advantage disappear. With his Aryan superiority rapidly evaporating, he left the meeting, fuming.

Immediately after, General Magli had another meeting, this one with Colonel Paul Colonna D'Istria, the local resistance leader with connections to the French Committee of National Liberation. The general assured him that all political prisoners would be immediately freed and that all the weapons and ammunition that had been intercepted and stored in the Italian arsenals would be released to them. There was a growing realization that they might soon be fighting side by side. However, there still was a problem.

Although some of the automatic weapons were British or American, most were either German- or Italian-made weapons that had been captured during the battles in North Africa, and no Corsican knew how to operate them. It was agreed they would be used only under the supervision of Italian officers, who would instruct the Corsican patriots on how to use them.

Soon after that meeting, two important messages, both addressed to the entire Italian armed forces, including the troops in Corsica, were received. One, from the new Italian prime minister, Pietro Badoglio, read: "The Italian government, recognizing the impossibility of continuing the unequal struggle against the overwhelming power of the enemy, and with the object of avoiding further and more grievous harm to our nation, has requested an armistice from General Eisenhower, commander in chief of the Anglo-American Allied forces. This request has been granted. The Italian forces will cease all acts of hostility against the Anglo-American forces, wherever they may be. They will, however, oppose attacks from any other forces."

The other message read: "This is General Dwight D. Eisenhower, commander in chief of the Allied forces. The Italian government has surrendered its armed forces unconditionally. As Allied commander in chief, I have granted a military armistice, the terms of which have been approved by the governments of the United Kingdom, the United States, and the Union of Soviet Socialist Republics. Thus, I am acting in the interests of the united nations. The Italian government has bound itself to abide by these terms without reservation. The armistice was signed by my representative and the representative of Marshal Badoglio, and it becomes effective this instant. Hostilities between the armed forces of the United Nations and those of Italy terminate at once. All Italians who now act to help eject the German aggressor from Italian soil will have the assistance and the support of the united nations."

These were encouraging promises, but one phrase left the Italian troops in Corsica puzzled, as they were not included in Eisenhower's statement. They were not on Italian soil; in reality, they were on French soil.

What, specifically, were they to do? What was their new role? How were they to know?

The answer to these questions came quickly and abruptly. In the middle of the night the troops were awakened with alarming news. The Germans, in a sneak attack, had opened fire on the unsuspecting Italian troops in charge of the port of Bastia. Without provocation, they set aflame the Italian ship *Humanitas* and the torpedo boat *Ardito*, killing fifteen sailors and twelve militiamen and claiming possession of the port.

At one o'clock in the morning, when General Magli received the news of this vile attack, he ordered all artillery available, including a battalion of anti-tank half-tracks, to counter attack, and by eight o'clock in the morning they had regained possession of the port. The quick reaction to this wanton act turned out to be a costly one for the Germans. By the time it was over, some five hundred Germans had lost their lives at sea, and with the valuable help of brave Corsican patriots, another couple of hundred were killed or wounded on land.

This immediate and successful response demonstrated two things: first, the Italians wouldn't allow the Germans to take control of Corsica; and second, they had shown the Americans, the British, and the French forces that they had all the intentions of fully participating in the liberation of Corsica.

****

It was still morning when General von Senger, faced with the failed attempt of his troops, arrived at the Italian headquarters, requesting to see General Magli immediately. Wearing a typical stone-faced expression of negativity, he deplored what had happened, with the excuse that neither he nor the commander of the German navy knew anything about the incident. He apologetically promised that nothing similar would ever happen again.

General Magli listened with a grave expression on his face. He remained silent for a short while and then said, "I am accepting your apology but with a warning. We will not tolerate any acts of hostility to the Italian troops, and we will respond—force with force and fire with fire."

General Magli no longer trusted von Senger, and immediately after the German general's departure, Magli ordered the Friuli Division, under the command of General Cotronei, to concentrate around Bastia, and the Cremona Division. under General Primieri, to fortify the zone around Corte, the seat of General Headquarters.

General Magli knew that there were an additional seven thousand Germans in the neighboring island of Sardinia who wanted to cross Corsica and evacuate from Bastia to Italy. He also knew from past experience that the Germans had to be watched closely.

To support his convictions, on the morning of September 11, only three days after the declaration of the armistice, he received an order from the supreme commander of the armed forces based in

Italy, emphasized in capital letters: "CONSIDER THE GERMANS AS ENEMY."

At that point in time, that brief statement turned out to be the five words that changed the lives of the Italian troops in Corsica. This was the day when the war took a new direction—a day when history made an abrupt, tragic about-face. Yesterday's enemies were today's allies, and yesterday's allies were now enemies. Neither the American Stars and Stripes nor the British Union Jack was the Italians' enemy any longer; their enemy was the swastika of the Third Reich. Suddenly, they found themselves fighting a new war—an undeclared war against the real enemy of Italy: the Nazis.

Ironically, until the armistice was signed, they had not fired a single shot since the day the occupation began, but now, in order to liberate the island from the talons of Germany, they were about to shoot tons of ammunition and sacrifice many precious young lives. Nevertheless, without any plan or intent, they were at the crossroads of history. They would now be fighting with their new allies in order to defeat their new foe.

****

Although their dilemma was resolved with the armistice, Renzo and Adrienne had no opportunity to celebrate. His time was completely consumed with his duties. True to prediction, the Germans' exodus from Sardinia to Corsica began instantly. With the help of the Panzer Division that had gone south to escort and protect them, they moved quickly north from Bonifacio to Bastia, and on their way up, they fought and thrashed all opposition. At once, the entire east coast of the island became a bloody battlefield.

From the moment the German troops approached the Italians' positions, they felt the full impact of a violent encounter. The powerful 90th Panzer Division, which had wanted to get to Bastia at all costs, overpowered the Italian troops whose mission was to stop them. Only twenty-five miles from La Grande Maison, many of the company's troops were involved in the bloody battle. By the time it was over, the Germans had not only come out the winners but had been able to take two thousand Italian soldiers as prisoners.

The Italians later learned that the general commander of the Friuli

Division was among the missing. His mysterious disappearance left them without any directives—and in a state of shock. No one knew exactly what had become of him, but many unfavorable suppositions about him instantly sprung up among the troops. Some officers felt he was not as capable as the other generals and that he was openly questioning General Magli's decisions. There were rumors that, suddenly and conveniently, he had fallen ill, and being unable to receive the proper orders, the Italians were outmaneuvered by the cunning Marshal von Senger. Others suggested that the general commander didn't want to fight the Germans in the first place, and some others hinted that he, being a Nazi sympathizer who had up until then ruled his troops like a tyrant, had quit like a coward and joined the Germans willingly.

Renzo, Tonelli, and Nino didn't know what to believe, and they weren't willing to jump to any conclusions. There was also the possibility that other Nazi sympathizers had started the rumor with the intention of demoralizing the troops. Whatever the truth was, his disappearance caused a deep sense of humiliation and shame in the Italian soldiers. They were fighting bravely, giving the last ounce of their strength, trying to reestablish the respect and credibility they had lost, and the general commander had presumably stained their honor instead. Nevertheless, they continued to fight with the hope that their contribution in the effort to defeat the Nazis would clearly show their desire to return Italy to the society of free nations and that their cooperation would increase the consideration of the Allies and improve the terms of the armistice.

Fortunately, immediately after this strange episode, General Magli appointed General Ugo De Lorenzis to take charge of their division, and quickly they began the march toward regaining their scope, pride, and much-needed self-esteem.

19 *The War in Corsica*

Two fierce battles took place in just as many days—battles that left the Italian troops exhausted. Renzo made countless trips to the field hospitals, transporting the dead and wounded soldiers from all companies, not just his. His ambulance narrowly escaped several shots from mortars as he sped along the pothole-damaged roads. The Germans were getting impatient and anxious. While the Germans were trying to get out of a dangerous country and avoid the consequences of a confrontation with their new enemy, the Italians were safely ensconced in a now-receptive territory, surrounded by freshly acquired allies.

The German strength was quickly dissipating, while the weakness of the Italians was steadily fading away. In addition, while the Germans were losing hope, the Italians, with the assignment of General De Lorenzis, noticed their hope grow. The more the fight intensified, the more their determination to defeat the Germans and drive them out of the island increased. The Italians knew the territory well, so as each German group tried to enter the main roads where the Italians had established positions, the Germans suffered great losses. In many cases, in order to expedite their exodus to Bastia to join the other Germans, they rendered inoperable or even destroyed large amounts of their own equipment and abandoned it. They also abandoned eight hundred of their men, who were promptly taken prisoner. Still, the Germans continued fighting; their manpower was still overwhelming. They fought so tenaciously that at one point, in order not to unnecessarily sacrifice any more lives from either side, a cease-fire was negotiated.

Immediately after, a letter was dropped from an airplane over the Italian headquarters. General von Senger requested from General Magli a restitution of the eight hundred German prisoners who had just been captured. With it came a menacing admonition that if the prisoners were not released by the following day, von Senger would order the execution of half of the three thousand Italian prisoners they held. Seventeen were from Renzo's company.

General Magli called his bluff. He knew that such an act would violate the Geneva Convention and von Senger wouldn't be so arrogant or stupid to defy that treaty. In fact, no German prisoners were restituted—and no Italian prisoners were executed.

The following day a new message from General von Senger reached General Magli's desk. It contained a proposal for a total exchange of prisoners within twenty-four hours. The proposal was accepted, and except for the wounded and the sick, all the German prisoners were promptly delivered. Unfortunately, however, General von Senger reneged on his promise. Only a fraction of the Italian prisoners were returned. General Magli issued a strong protest, to which von Senger never replied.

Three days later, von Senger sent two messengers with a letter demanding the return of their wounded. After what had already taken place, General Magli answered that such a request would not be considered. The messengers, carrying the white flag, returned to their camp in silence.

✳✳✳✳

While the Italian troops were fighting the potent, well-equipped Germans of the Reichsführer SS in the north, many important things were happening in the south of the island, politically and militarily. On the political side, the Corsican patriots seized control of the island and ousted the pro-Nazi Vichy government in Ajaccio and other centers, substituting it with a prefectural council. On the military side, American rangers landed on the beaches of Corsica. Two French cruisers, six destroyers, and three submarines helped land some French forces in Ajaccio, together with the first contingent of Moroccan troops.

The next day, General Martin, who had been assigned to reunite all incoming French troops in Corsica, and General Mallard, who had been named governor of the island, entered the port of Ajaccio.

Soon after, General Magli met with all the newly arrived commanders of the United Nations forces. A full, loyal collaboration of all troops involved was established. Italian light artillery and infantry regiments would participate. In addition, the entire Italian automotive department would assure the transportation of any Allied troops, wherever and whenever needed.

Initially, there were some disagreements regarding who would assume command of the operations, but after exchanging many opinions, General Magli reminded them of the real reason and the sole purpose of the meeting. He pointed out that the Italians had already had ten diverse fighting encounters with the Germans in three separate days, in which they had lost over three hundred men, and the blood of 161 Italian soldiers and nine officers had been spilled.

That said, he suggested that everyone abandon their personal pride and ambitions and only concentrate on their common goal: to defeat the Germans—quickly. At meeting's end it was agreed that each participating group would remain under the orders of their own commanders. General Magli was grateful to see his proposal accepted, but the possibility of some unknown disappointment still loomed.

****

On September 21, French general Henri Giraud, who commanded the twenty-five thousand French troops in North Africa and who was co-president with General Charles De Gaulle of the French Committee of National Liberation, arrived in Corsica.

He immediately met with General Magli at the Prefecture of Corte to discuss, in depth, some particulars regarding the Italian participation to the war effort. It was his opinion that because the Italian Friuli Division had suffered heavy losses of men and equipment, it would be wise to keep it out of danger and transfer what was left of the division to Sardinia.

This was a proposal General Magli could not accept. He maintained that his troops were young and resilient and could contribute whatever was asked of them. He knew his men well and was sure that such a decision would have a corrosive effect on their morale, as well as crushing their spirits and creating a great psychological collapse. All they needed at the moment was to be reorganized and have their weapons upgraded. They would be sure to respond with valor to whatever was asked of them.

General Giraud didn't insist, but at the end of the one-on-one meetings, it was concluded that the confrontation with General von Senger would begin immediately. Thus, with the sole aim of driving the Germans from the island and liberating Corsica, the French troops, Moroccans, and Corsican patriots, with assistance from the air by the British and Americans, joined the Italians in what was, for them, the third phase of operations.

And so, from Bastia to Casamozza, from Vezzani to Zonza, from the crossroads of San Leonard to the Teghime Pass, they all participated in shelling the German outposts by land and bombing their units by air.

The attacks continued for a few days at an accelerating pace until they reached a strong, unchained fury. The Moroccans, a fierce and fearless fighting group, gave their all. The partisans, under the capable hands of Colonel D'Istria, contributed valiantly.

The counterattack of the Germans was furious and bloody. Some of their soldiers fought with all their might, and some of them clearly showed that rather than retreat, they would prefer to die. And many of them did. But the vast majority chose the cowardly way out. They boarded any transport plane available, intending to get off the island, but few succeeded. The attack of the Allied air force was immediate, fruitful, and rewarding. An air blockade was established, the result of which was that within two days, long-range fighter planes shot down twenty-six German air transport planes carrying personnel and officers as they sought to run from Bastia to Livorno, Italy. At the same time, on the sea, a large number of boats were spotted by reconnaissance aircraft and attacked by British submarines. Even with strong German opposition, they sank ten ships and damaged five others.

And then the firing stopped. For a while, all was calm, silent, and peaceful.

One of the tasks assigned to the Italians was arduous and hazardous, but it was performed above and beyond everyone's expectations. They cleared every road of all the abandoned equipment. Every bridge that had been blown up by the fleeing Germans was repaired so that it was safe enough for the Allies to cross. And finally, every line of communication that had been disconnected by the Germans was quickly hooked up, even while the Italian troops were under fire. But their progress was slowed when they discovered that during the night, German airplanes had peppered the entire battle zone with booby traps consisting of fake wristwatches, which upon winding would explode, and cheap fountain pens that would detonate when one tried to write with them. These items were not intended to kill the finder but to render him unable to fight and in need of assistance, thus eliminating his helpers as well. But that bait, as clever as it was, didn't work. Only two soldiers fell victim to their own curiosity. Fortunately, they escaped with only minor injuries on their fingers.

During this time, Renzo pushed the limits of his old ambulance to the point that it was in dire need of repairs, and he requested permission to return to La Grande Maison. Since his ambulance was not the only one on the front line, permission was granted.

Adrienne had been constantly on his mind. It had been nearly two weeks since he'd seen her, and he felt that his thoughts of their future was the main reason for his survival. He needed to be with her again, to tell her how much he loved her, and to hear her echo his sentiments. Her presence would erase, or at least soften, the impact of the gruesome events he had witnessed. He needed her now.

20 *Vows*

On the night of September 21, Renzo climbed the hill to the hut to see if Adrienne was there. They hadn't seen each other since September 8, the day they learned about the armistice. Too much time had passed. He missed her dearly and had to see her.

She was there, looking more beautiful and radiant than ever, and although she was at the beginning of the fourth month of her pregnancy, she was barely showing. Renzo noticed contentment in her eyes, which to him was a silent admission of her happiness for not having gone through with the abortion. They were grateful to God for having given them a way out of the huge mountain of problems they'd faced only a few weeks earlier.

As they hugged and kissed, Renzo was haunted by mental anguish caused by the horrifying events he had witnessed. He felt sick to his stomach and in a state of deep agitation. He had transported too many wounded soldiers to the various field hospitals to be mended; he had taken too many dead soldiers to an improvised morgue where their bodies waited to be decently and honorably buried in nearby cemeteries.

He could neither absorb nor accept everything that had occurred. Renzo collapsed on a bale of hay, drained of his strength. He broke out in sweat and unsuccessfully tried to explain his feelings to Adrienne—"So many men ... so much blood ... my friends ... my comrades ..."—but Renzo was still shell-shocked and the words didn't come. He began to weep uncontrollably with loud and unrestrained sobs.

Adrienne, deeply concerned to see him in such a pitiful condition, knelt beside him and hugged him tightly, stroking his hair and gently kissing his cheek. Words failed her, too, but she tried to comfort him. "You're here now, with me. You're safe. I love you so much."

He returned her hug, although he knew he wasn't safe—not there and definitely not out on the battlefield. The mortars had struck too close, and the explosions still reverberated in his ears. All he could think was that he, too, was vulnerable, and he saw the specter of death advancing threateningly in his direction. He realized how vulnerable he now looked, how weak he might appear to Adrienne as she tried to console him. The fact that he needed consoling made him feel that he had lost all the courage he once possessed. Even the caresses from her smooth hands didn't help to steady his trembling arms.

Renzo then instinctively looked deeply into Adrienne's eyes, took a deep breath, and in an emotionally loaded whisper asked, "Will you marry me, Adrienne?"

The urgency of that unexpected proposal startled her, but her reply was immediate. "Yes," she responded with fervor. "I want to marry you. I intend to marry you but when the war is over—not until you are a private citizen again."

"That may be too long a wait. The conflict in Corsica may end soon, but this war will not be over for a long time," Renzo said.

"But didn't you tell me you believed the war would be over soon when we were discussing …" Adrienne patted her stomach with both her hands.

"Yes, I believed it then, but the events that have happened since have made everything so unpredictable now."

She looked at him and caressed his brow with her nimble fingers, as an assuring sign of understanding and support. "I will wait for you, then."

Renzo felt she didn't truly understand how much the situation had worsened in Italy. He needed to explain. "Let me tell you what I understand about what has been happening." He took her hand and led her to a bale of hay, where they sat. "There have been so many developments that I'm not sure where to begin. German paratroopers have liberated Benito Mussolini from his prison at the Gran Sasso. He formed a new Fascist Republic with the intention of remaining loyal to the Third Reich. And now Italy is divided—half of it occupied by the destructive Germans and half being bombed and devastated by the liberating Allied forces.

"When the Corsican campaign is over, there will no longer be the need of Italian troops here. I understand we will be transferred to Sardinia for a period of recovery and reorganization, and then eventually we will be sent to southern Italy to join the Allied forces for the liberation and reunification of my own country. Now, do you see why I want to marry you this very moment? Things are so uncertain that by then, you might be waiting for my ghost."

"But how?" she asked. "We have no priest, no witnesses."

"Yes, we do," Renzo replied. "God is our priest."

"I see," she said, somewhat puzzled. "And the witnesses?"

Renzo looked at her, his eyes moist. "We have witnesses." Impulsively, he wrapped his arm around her waist and escorted her outside. He found it appropriate that they should, for the third time, visit her parents' grave. "Here are our witnesses," he said. "Now, let's proceed."

And without wavering, they knelt at the foot of the cold granite tombstone to declare their vows. Adrienne hesitated for a second; she looked at the heavens and then at the tomb and said, "In front of you, my dearest parents, and in the eyes of God, I marry my beloved Renzo Crespi, with the solemn promise that I will love him today, tomorrow, and forever."

"With God's blessing and your consent," Renzo echoed, "I, Renzo Crespi, marry your daughter, Adrienne Santi, and promise to dedicate my life to her and to love, respect, and cherish her until the end of time."

Trembling, they stood up and, as if coached by an invisible prompter, said in unison, "And now we pronounce ourselves husband and wife."

They had no rings to exchange but tenderly fell into each other's arms as if it were their first embrace … or maybe their last. Neither found any words to say, but their eyes seemed to be communicating in their own language. With their limbs still trembling, partly from the fear of the uncertainty of today, partly for the hope of tomorrow, and partly out of sheer trepidation, they returned to the hut.

Once there, completely oblivious to the fleeting time, they celebrated the purest and sincerest expression of their love. And when he left her, descending the hill on his way to La Grande Maison, he feared nothing. He now felt he could face, accept, and conquer anything that came his way.

21 *The New Boots*

Renzo chatted with the mechanic from the motor pool as he checked out Renzo's aging and overused ambulance.

"It needs some serious work. Tires, plugs, filters, all your fluids. Looks like this thing went through a war."

They both forced a laugh, and the mechanic walked away to get some tools.

As Renzo waited, he recognized Lieutenant Semprefedele's whistling as he approached from behind.

"How's your ambulance?" the lieutenant asked.

"Needs some work. Nardoni's a good mechanic. He'll get it as good as new in no time."

Semprefedele walked around the ambulance, looking up and down as if he were about to buy it. Returning to Renzo's side, he gave him a look of mixed curiosity and puzzlement. "What's this I hear about you wanting a new pair of boots?" he asked. It had obviously come to the lieutenant's attention that Renzo had unsuccessfully requisitioned the quartermaster for a pair of boots, either new or rebuilt, several times.

Renzo looked at him for a moment and simply raised his right foot, like a horse ready to be shod, and showed him the gaping hole in the sole of his boot. "I have repeatedly requested a new pair, sir, but the only response I get is 'Our stock has been depleted. If or when we get new supplies, you'll be the first in line.'"

The lieutenant furrowed his brow, frowned, and nodded. He looked at Renzo with such intensity that Renzo clearly saw the anguish and remorse of a good officer who was pained to know his subordinates were lacking necessary items. Lieutenant Semprefedele gave Renzo a benevolent wink of assurance, clasped his hands behind his back and, as if pretending not to have heard Renzo's comments, changed the subject.

"You realize the French artillery has not yet arrived in Corsica."

"Yes, sir."

"We've been assigned to give artillery cover to four battalions of Moroccan troops and fully cooperate with them on an imminent major assault on the German lines. General Louchet, commander of the French Colonial Infantry, will be in charge of the attack. We will leave at sundown to reach them, and I need you to leave in the morning, as soon as the ambulance is fixed." That said, he turned around and took one step but then stopped, as if he had just remembered something. "Oh, Crespi. You *will* get your boots," he said. "I promise!" He pursed his lips, resumed whistling "The Toreador Song" from *Carmen*, and walked away.

****

The following morning, the strong scent of new leather awoke Renzo. A pair of new boots rested neatly under his cot, begging to be worn. They were shiny, soft and pliable, and masterfully crafted. Looking closer, Renzo realized they were officers boots. Lieutenant Semprefedele had kept his promise.

That morning, with the ambulance repaired, Renzo sped along to the front lines. He soon slowed down when he came upon a man who was drinking from a canteen with one hand and hitching a ride with the other. The man staggered, nearly tripping over his own feet, and tunelessly sang in a sort of unreal joy, the joy that comes out of a bottle of rum. Renzo didn't want to stop, but the men had been ordered to cooperate and give assistance without hesitation to any and all French troops who requested it. At first, Renzo wasn't sure where the man was from, but as he got nearer he could see the man was dressed in a brown-and-gray striped hooded coat with a red sash wrapped around his waist. The hood was down, and he wore a large turban, out of which protruded a greasy, unkempt black mane. Renzo determined the man was a Moroccan goumier, an auxiliary soldier who supported the French.

Renzo pulled the ambulance alongside the road and waited as the Moroccan approached the vehicle. "Where are you going?" Renzo asked.

"Saint Florent," he said.

"That's where I'm going. Get in."

Unlike other vehicles, the ambulance had removable doors of Plexiglas framed in steel and wood, to be used in case of inclement weather. But it was a beautiful, bright day, and no doors were needed. For safety reasons, however, in order to protect the driver and the passenger from sliding off the seat, a leather covered steel chain crossed the opening where the door would have been.

"Come in, come in!" Renzo urged. "I have no time to waste."

The man jumped in and, with a sigh of relief, made himself comfortable. He was small and wiry, with a dark, unshaven face that was caked with a crust of crud. His hands were splattered with a layer of dry mud, and his garments soiled, as if he had slept all night under a chestnut tree. He was the filthiest man Renzo had ever seen. His eyes were flaming red, either from lack of sleep or an excessive ingestion of rum. His carbine was dusty, and a long dagger hung on a ragged canvas bandolier, half out of its scabbard. As the Moroccan slid onto the seat, a peculiar, acrid smell followed him. It pierced Renzo's nostrils, causing his nose to curl up. He picked up speed, hoping to ventilate the cab, but the smell hung on to the Moroccan. At first, Renzo thought that the stench was the result of poor hygiene. From time to time, with a sizable dose of curiosity and an equal amount of fear, he sneaked glances at the stranger seated alongside him. Eventually, he spotted a small wire hoop hanging from a black leather belt, just below the sash. What at first appeared to be a dozen or so half-dried mushrooms were strung on the hoop. But they weren't mushrooms. They were, as the man explained to Renzo in a mixture of grunts, bad French, and hand motions, ears that he had cut off dead German soldiers—soldiers he killed a couple of days earlier that were now decomposing.

To the Moroccan, they were precious trophies, but Renzo was outraged, and he was convinced that this animal had no notion of civilization. Renzo tried to hide the distaste he had developed for his passenger, but he couldn't. The stench of rotting human flesh sickened him. He stopped the ambulance and leaned his head over the side, the victim of a long-lasting, severe attack of retching.

Renzo resumed driving in absolute silence. The Moroccan appeared to be unconcerned. He continued to grin and tug and twirl his long black mustache, while eyeing Renzo with his black, bloodshot eyes.

Renzo was so incensed, he wanted to kick him out of the ambulance but didn't, being more concerned with the order to assist any Allied soldier. However, as he drove, cursing the moment he had stopped to pick up the soldier, a chill of fear assaulted him. He noticed from the corner of his eyes that the filthy soldier's heavy stare was fixed on his feet. At first, Renzo assumed that the movements of his feet fascinated the soldier—the poor condition of the road required him to continually change gears and switch from brakes to clutch and vice versa—but he soon discovered otherwise. Using his crude method of communication and equally poor French, the man made his desires known.

"Boots nice. I take."

"Excuse me?"

"I take boots."

"Listen, we're on the same side now. We're fighting the Germans together. We're not enemies."

The Moroccan let out a threatening-sounding laugh. "You give boots, or I take boots and feet." With that, he removed his dagger from the scabbard and pointed it at Renzo's throat. "I kill you *and* take boots!"

"You don't really mean that. We're allies. We have a common cause to defeat the Germans."

"Stop car now!" he screamed. "Give boots or die."

Renzo was petrified. He knew that the Moroccan would follow through with his threat, but instead of applying the brakes to stop or even to slow down, Renzo accelerated to a speed much too dangerous for the narrow and dusty road. It was unsafe and treacherous, with deep ruts and large potholes caused by the continuous stream of both the German and Italian armored cars.

A dense forest of cork trees lined the left side of the road, while on the right, a menacing, steep, rocky gorge plunged into a shallow, churning river. Any error or misjudgment by Renzo would surely be fatal. His head was in tumult and yet, suddenly, the seeds of self-preservation germinated and took root in his mind. He had traveled that road many times and knew it well. He knew that he would soon reach a long stretch of straight road, and after that, a sharp left turn that quickly and steadily climbed to the top of the mountain, only to emerge on a plateau of uncultivated flat land.

This was a ray of hope, but it would be his only chance. He had to act rationally and quickly. The Moroccan was still brandishing his dagger with a clear intent to use it when Renzo, pretending to have resigned to his will, began to slow down. As Renzo looked at this crazed soldier, he noticed that the safety chain on the passenger door was unhooked. Instantly, he thought of a plan. This was the break he had hoped for. He was no longer afraid.

Renzo pressed the accelerator pedal to the floor causing his passenger to snap back, whipping his head against the steel backboard. The blow forced his turban to slide over his eyes, blocking his vision. He tried to readjust it but lost grip of his dagger, sending it flying out the door. Renzo's ambulance reached breakneck speed. He no longer heard the crazy beast's deafening shouts, and as he approached the center of the hairpin turn, he held on to the steering wheel and stomped down on the brakes. The ambulance swerved violently, like a furious snake in the dust, and came perilously closer to the jagged edge of the cliff. When the vehicle finally came to a screeching stop, the dazed Moroccan's head slammed against the hard dashboard, stunning him even more. He groped blindly to reach something, anything he could hang onto for support. He reached across the front seat and grabbed for Renzo, who managed to evade him. Cramped in the limited space of the cab, Renzo clung to the steering wheel and pivoted on the seat to face him. Now there was alarm and fear on the Moroccan's face, but Renzo didn't care.

He bent his knees to his chest and rammed his feet into the Moroccan's chest. Desperate, the man swung his fist at Renzo, but that increased Renzo's advantage because the man had created a stronger leverage in Renzo's legs. Instinctively, Renzo summoned his strength. Still trembling with fear and anger but with renewed vigor, Renzo shoved the Moroccan headfirst out of the ambulance. The Moroccan tumbled down the deep, jagged precipice. Renzo heard a blood-curdling scream, along with the sound of rocks falling down the cliff and into the river.

And then, silence.

All Renzo could hear was the purring sound of the newly reconditioned engine of the ambulance. It was over. He had survived. Was the Moroccan dead or alive? Renzo didn't know. All he knew was that he still had his new boots and his feet. Not to mention his ears.

22 *An Unexpected Return*

Although there had been some artillery exchanges over the next few days on the mountainous terrain of the front line, nothing of significance had been achieved. There were neither advances nor retreats on either side. The company waited for all the groups to join them for a strong and final push into Bastia.

The Moroccan incident was still vivid in Renzo's mind while driving his ambulance on the tortuous, steep hill on his way to Bastia to exchange supplies with his counterpart there. As sunset approached, he spotted a stooped-over, dazed figure of a man. Dressed in a soiled German sailor uniform, and carrying an overcoat, the man staggered up the hill, slightly hunched forward. He appeared to have trouble catching his breath. On hearing the sound of the engine, he scrambled off the edge of the road and into the thick chestnut orchard. Renzo followed with caution. When he was parallel to the man, he stopped, shut off the engine, and removed the keys. Gun in hand, he exited the ambulance.

"Halt!" he ordered. "Turn around and raise your hands."

Renzo expected the man to attempt an escape. Instead, the man turned and almost immediately, he gently placed the coat on the ground and rushed in Renzo's direction, not with hands up but with trembling arms wide open, as if he wanted to embrace him.

Puzzled and with his gun still pointed at the man, Renzo retreated, still studying him as he continued toward Renzo. He found nothing recognizable about the pathetic-looking German sailor who pretended to know him. His unshaven, puffed-up face was plastered with a mixture of blood, dust, and finely crushed road gravel. He looked desolate and desperate, and his eyes, blackened and bulging, made him appear as if he had been the loser in a boxing match. His nose was severely scratched, and his bloodied lips were badly swollen.

He tried speaking to Renzo, but his voice came out harsh and guttural, making him sound like a Neanderthal. His words were incomprehensible at first, but then he cleared his throat and repeated, "Renzo, my son. Renzo, my son. God has sent you to rescue me!"

Renzo was startled that the man had said his name and further taken aback when the man stood directly in front of him, said his name again, and embraced him. Although oddly moved by the stranger's actions, Renzo still wondered who he was and how he knew his name. Seconds later, it all made sense. Gently pushing him away, Renzo looked at him intently. With a mixture of joy and pain, he realized that the sad, grotesque caricature of the man standing in front of him was the same man who had provided him with many moments of laughter, the same man who, notwithstanding his personality flaws, character weaknesses, and shortcomings, Renzo had grown to respect—Captain Francesco Maria Giancarlo Benelli.

So much in him had changed; so much of him was missing. The crisply pressed uniform he was so proud of was replaced by a filthy, motor-oil-stained German sailor's uniform. Instead of his perennially polished knee-high boots, his feet were in a pair of worn-out sandals. His monocle, the mark of his lofty civility, was gone and so was his symbol of security and power—his priceless horsewhip.

On seeing what was left of the once-proud old soldier, Renzo felt a sense of infinite compassion for him. The fact that he had called him "my son," plus the high regard Renzo had for him, both as an officer and a father figure, compelled Renzo to hug him. And as they embraced, he felt the difference of rank between them disappear. They were equal now, and as equals, Renzo granted himself the liberty to ask for some pertinent explanations.

"What's happened to you, and what are you doing in a German sailor uniform? Are you a deserter?"

Benelli shook his head. "No."

"How did you get like this?" Renzo asked as he began to remove the mud from Benelli's face with a wet towel and patch the cuts and bruises on his brow and nose.

Gasping for breath, Benelli explained, "After I left the company, I was sent to a month-long intensive rehabilitation program." The captain winced as Renzo applied an antiseptic to his cuts. "When that was completed, I was assigned the command of a small infantry company near Ajaccio. All was well for a while, but when the hostilities against the Germans erupted, my company and I were taken prisoner by the Germans and brought to the Bastia Citadel." The captain took a deep breath as Renzo completed his work. "A few days later, the Italian and German commanders agreed to exchange prisoners. But when the exchange took place, some of the Italian prisoners had not been returned. I was among the many who remained."

He stopped talking and brushed tears from his eyes. Renzo gave him a drink of water from his canteen. When Benelli regained his composure, he continued. "Last night I bargained with a greedy German guard. I managed to keep some personal items from being confiscated, and they came to good use. I offered him my gold wristwatch for a complete sailor uniform. I gave him my diamond-studded golden ring to leave the exit gate open and my silver cigarette lighter for a pair of boots. When dawn arrived, I managed to escape undetected and walked away, hoping to reach La Grande Maison. At one point, it looked as though luck were with me. I heard the sputtering engine of a truck coming up a hill at a snail's pace, and I thought I recognized it as one of the company's trucks.

"Because I was wearing a German uniform and didn't want to be run over, I didn't try to hitch a ride. Instead, I hid behind a bush, waiting for the truck to go by so I would be able to jump on it without being detected. That turned out to be a mistake. As the truck slowly passed, I ran from behind the bush and leaped to take hold of the tailgate of the vehicle. As I pulled myself up, I could see it was heavily filled with war *matériel*. I didn't see any escort aboard, so I decided to climb in. I had one leg in when a lone soldier emerged from behind the crates. Obviously, he thought I was a German soldier. The next thing I knew, he struck me on the head with the butt of his rifle. I tried to convince him that I was an Italian officer, but the soldier wouldn't listen. He kept hitting me. The soldier smashed the rifle butt into my head and face and then my shoulders and upper arms and lastly my hands that were gripping the gate. The pain was so excruciating that I couldn't hang on anymore and finally, with broken fingers and a dented skull, I had to let go. I fell and rolled on the gravel-filled, dusty ground. Not long after, I saw your ambulance and knew I was safe."

"Yes, sir," Renzo said. "You are safe, but you need more help than I can give you. I must take you to the hospital. For now," he said, placing both hands on Benelli's shoulders and giving a slight squeeze of assurance, "I'll give you something to eat."

The captain mumbled something, but Renzo couldn't hear what he said. Renzo walked to the rear of the ambulance and found a congealed ration of meat in with the supplies. He kept glancing at the captain, who was pacing at the side of the ambulance. The captain, feverishly and somewhat agitated, retrieved his coat and removed something very familiar from a large inside pocket—something that Renzo knew he cherished more than anything else. It was the only link that he carried with him from the glorious life of yesterday up to the misery of the present, the sole memento his father had given him—the ibex horn. It was still wrapped in the chamois cloth, and at once he began to polish it with the same passionate affection as Renzo had seen him do many times. He must have taken great pains to keep it hidden from his captors.

Renzo continued to prepare the captain's food, leaving him undisturbed to enjoy what was a sacred routine for him. Suddenly, the ambulance rocked to one side as if it had been forcibly pushed by a strong gust of wind. Renzo heard a loud scream, followed by a thud.

And then ... silence.

He quickly ran around the ambulance to see what had happened, and a terrible shiver went through him. To his horror, he saw Captain Benelli lying on the ground, writhing in pain, with the ibex horn at his side, its tip bloodied. Apparently, he had placed the base of the trophy against the side of the ambulance with the sharp tip of the horn on his bare stomach and lunged on it with all his weight, with the intent to kill himself. Fortunately, he failed.

With a closer look, Renzo noticed that the horn had made a

relatively shallow puncture wound and had not penetrated deep enough to damage any vital organs. It seemed that it had barely passed the skin and the fat tissues of the abdomen.

Renzo helped Benelli get into the front seat of the ambulance. He bandaged the wound as best as he could and, without asking Benelli's consent, headed for the field hospital. The captain needed hospital treatment anyway from the wounds received at the hands of the soldier on the truck, and this act of madness only made it more necessary. Renzo could explain the captain's German uniform to the officials there. As he drove away, he eyed the captain with sidelong glances, wondering what could prompt any man to behave that way. *Perhaps the captain reached the limit of his emotional stability,* he thought. *Perhaps he could no longer tolerate his physical humiliation.* Whatever the reason, all Renzo could see sitting beside him was a quivering wreck of a man, shattered by a scrambled, disturbed mind.

They remained silent for a long while but then, filled with deep compassion, Renzo asked, "Whatever tempted you to do such a thing, anyway?"

Captain Benelli looked at Renzo with a vacant stare and then slowly spoke. "I wanted to be a good—no, a great—captain. A great officer. Perhaps some of my visions and plans for the troops and some of my tactics were a bit misguided. I see that now. Looking back at them, I am filled with shame and fear. Shame, because in some ways I have come to look foolish, a laughingstock to some of my peers. And ultimately, I feared being court-martialed as a war criminal for some of my acts. I may be over-thinking this, but I've done many things since we arrived in Corsica for which I am no longer proud."

He took a deep breath. "I'm sure you remember the incident with the old shepherd when we first arrived. I treated him miserably, for no reason other than my own pride. And how I took advantage of my rank with the Santis. I terrorized some poor women who were only reciting the rosary. And worst of all, I prohibited Padre Silvestri from ringing the church bells because of my own paranoia. I treated the men, including you, abusively at times, simply to flaunt my rank. I did the same with the Santis, who treated me with great hospitality."

Renzo considered the possibility that Monsieur Santi may have actually used the captain's pomposity to gain information. There was no need for him to know about any of that, however, as the situation was now different.

The captain continued. "Those are just the more insignificant local abuses of power of which I am guilty. As an officer, I am ashamed of not being victorious against the Germans." Pausing again, he thought of the events of the day. "And even worse, I will forever bear the disgrace of having worn, just for my own survival, a German sailor's uniform. I am a coward."

"But, sir, in my opinion, all these things are of minor importance when placed in the entire context of this war. I would think they would not be considered for prosecution by the military tribunal and surely not worthy of being remembered by the Corsicans."

But the captain's agitated mind continued to magnify his fears to the point that he was no longer listening.

It was long past sunset when they arrived at the field hospital. Renzo explained to the doctor in charge that the captain had received his wounds at the hands of a soldier on the truck after making his escape in the German uniform. He added that in the captain's confused state, he had accidentally fallen over the horn. As Renzo was leaving, he reassured the captain with a solemn promise that he would return soon.

****

As he had promised, Renzo visited Captain Benelli in the field hospital. Twenty-four beds were lined up in two rows in the partitioned section, separating the recovering soldiers from the triage section and operating room. Pulling aside the curtain at the recovery room's entrance, Renzo looked down the rows of beds. When he saw the captain, although only two days had passed, Renzo was immediately convinced that Benelli was well on his way to a complete recovery. Renzo quickly walk toward him and stood at the foot of the bed. Benelli was lying in his bed, still hurting from the puncture wound and the beating he'd taken, but the swelling of his face had almost disappeared. A pinkish hue covered his now-relaxed, clean-shaven face, and there was no sadness in his eyes. His voice was no longer feeble and fading; it was now strong and clear.

"Renzo, come closer." The captain motioned for Renzo to sit in a chair adjacent to the bed. Renzo edged the chair nearer to the bed and placed a sack he was carrying on the floor. The captain took Renzo's hand and squeezed it as tightly as he could. "I'm so fortunate that I stumbled upon you in my time of need. You saved my life."

"Sir, I'm just happy I was able to help." Renzo looked around to make sure no one was listening. "And no one knows about … your wound."

"Yes. Thank you for your discretion. I don't know what came over me."

"You had been through a lot. More than most men. The mind is fragile."

"It is. But thank you again."

Renzo reached for the sack. "I tried to clean it up for you." He reached in the sack and took out the ibex trophy, wrapped in the chamois.

Benelli's eyes widened, he trembled, and tears of joy streamed down his face.

"I hope I did a good enough job for you."

"It's perfect. I didn't know what had happened to it. I was so confused at the time." With a silent motion of his hands, he invited Renzo to come near him for an embrace. They remained heart to heart for a while, the captain patting Renzo's back. "Thank you again for visiting. And for this," he said, holding the horn tenderly. "Tomorrow morning I will be flown to a civilian hospital in Sardinia where I'll stay for a while. The doctors found some light fractures in my arms and in one of my legs."

"I'm sorry to hear that, Captain." Renzo extended his hand. "I hope it's not the case, but if this is the last time I see you, best wishes for a new life after the war."

The captain took Renzo's hand and pulled him close for another embrace. "I wish you the same, Renzo."

As they said their good-byes, a thought flashed through Renzo's mind. What did the future hold for the captain? Would he climb the military ladder? Could he move on to colonel and then general, or would he be perceived as damaged goods and get lost in the system? Renzo concluded that whatever Benelli's fate, he would forever remember the captain as his favorite commanding officer, whom he profoundly respected and whose camaraderie he would always cherish.

"May God bless you, sir," Renzo said, with a lump in his throat. He stiffened and saluted the captain with the most formal salute he had ever given any officer. Trembling with emotion, he turned to leave.

As he reached the curtain doorway, the captain called, "Renzo, wait."

"Yes, sir. What is it?"

The captain's arm was extended toward Renzo. He was holding the ibex horn. "My father gave this to me. I have cherished it for many years. A lifetime spent in the military left me no time for a wife or children. You have been as close to a son as I will ever have. I want you to have this. I know it will be in good hands. Pass it on to your son when the time comes."

"Sir, no. I couldn't."

"I insist. My last order to you as your superior officer. You don't want to be court-martialed, do you?"

"No, sir." They both laughed. Renzo took the horn and held it out. "I always admired it when I saw it on your desk, and I know how much it means to you. I will treasure it forever."

"Now go. And thank you again."

"Good-bye, sir."

When Renzo reached the corridor and the curtain door closed behind him, he paused, leaned against the wall, and wondered how long it would take him to overcome the traumatic roller-coaster experience of the past few days. But he didn't have to wait long. In the blink of an eye, his sadness quickly changed into joy. A familiar noise, as pleasant and welcome as the greeting of an old friend, jolted Renzo from his negative thoughts. He heard Captain Giancarlo Maria Francesco Benelli sneeze … uncontrollably.

23 *Renzo's Twenty-First Birthday*

The last few days in September turned out to be most rewarding and very encouraging. The Allied forces had formed a powerful front in a horseshoe formation around the city of Bastia and the airport in Borgo—the last stronghold of the remaining Germans. Although from the brow of the surrounding hills they had a definite control of the situation, they were not immune to the counter-offense of the Nazi troops. And as the intensity of the operation increased, the number of wounded and dead continually mounted. Renzo had long since weathered his first encounter with death, but he hadn't developed any callousness for it.

He continued to run from La Grande Maison to the front lines and from there to the various field hospitals, or to one of the sixteen existing infirmaries, or to whichever medical assistance centers were available.

It seemed that his life had become a routine. Every day was the same as yesterday or the day before—except that this was the first day of October; Renzo's twenty-first birthday, a day in which he should have become mature enough to separate the exhaustion of war and death from the joy of life and peace. Oddly enough, he realized it hadn't been war that had matured him. Adrienne and her love had done that.

The day had begun in a sort of a restrained, happy mood. Tonelli had gathered the few remaining soldiers at La Grande Maison, and for the first time, the guitar music blended in the morning air while the entire group joined in singing the tunes of birthday wishes.

Renzo had brought the ibex trophy out to show everyone. He said it was an early birthday gift from Captain Benelli. Renzo felt that no one needed to know the fatherly sentiment Benelli had expressed to him, nor the captain's attempt to use the horn against himself.

In spite of the overall festive atmosphere of the day, a cloud of disquiet hovered above Renzo's head—a cloud that stubbornly followed him all day long like his shadow. He worried about Benelli's fate; if he could reconcile his past problems and emerge a new and better man. And he fretted over his own future, wondering where he would go from here and how long before he could return. He constantly tried to clear his mind by diverting his thoughts to Adrienne and reliving some of their most intimate moments but to no avail. The cloud of anxiety was unwilling to leave him alone, not even toward the end of the day when he discovered that the news of his birthday had spread around the village. He suspected that Corinne had something to do with it because as soon as evening fell, she and a few elderly women from the neighborhood, accompanied by Padre Silvestri, crossed the gate and came in bringing large trays containing all sorts of chestnut-based cookies and biscuits and various Corsican dishes.

At that moment, he thought he felt as happy as he could be, but then, to his great joy, he saw Adrienne crossing the gate, accompanied by her faithful Domenica. She came directly to him and as he went to greet her, she curtsied delicately, and demurely extended her hand, expressing good wishes for his future.

This marked the first time that they were outdoors together in the presence of other people, and Renzo was so happy that it took all his emotional strength to resist the temptation to hold her in his arms and shout out loud that they were in love. But discretion was still called for. He realized that the preservation of her honor was more important than the declaration of their love.

Renzo took the opportunity to show her the ibex trophy, explaining the fatherly gesture extended by Captain Benelli. "There's more to the story," he whispered. "I'll tell you the first chance we get. Why don't we sit with the others over there?" He motioned toward the chestnut tree, where the rest of the revelers were singing along with Tonelli's guitar playing. Adrienne carried the trophy and held it as they settled down with the others. She sat clutching the trophy, admiring it.

They all sat for a while on the circular cement base under the tree, exchanging niceties and singing, but just when they thought they had reached the apex of the festivities, the ominous sound of an approaching airplane silenced everyone. The Corsican folk songs they were singing stopped.

They thought at first that the sound might be coming from an American or a British reconnaissance airplane, but they soon recognized the unmistakable roar of a light German plane. Everyone rose, and instinctively, the soldiers responsible for the anti-aircraft weaponry ran to their positions. Nino and Tonelli stood with the remaining soldiers and watched, along with Renzo, who was trying to speak to Adrienne at the top of his voice, trying to be heard over the sound of the plane.

"You and Domenica need to go back to the house!" He barely got the words out. Within seconds, several flares tied to parachutes came from the sky, brightly illuminating a large area of terrain. In no time, a machine gun began spraying bullets at them and at the trucks lined up on the road alongside them. Screaming with fear, the women scattered away at once to the safety of their own homes. Renzo grabbed Adrienne, who was still holding the ibex trophy, and huddled with her and Domenica next to the large tree. Fortunately, the first pass had no effect on them. No one was hurt; nothing had been hit. But the plane came back again, and by this time, the soldiers manning the anti-aircraft batteries were ready. With the aid of a couple of large spotlights, they began shooting at the plane.

"Adrienne! Leave now! Run home! This is no place for you to be," Renzo begged, but she refused to move.

"Wherever you are is where I want to be," she said.

"Domenica, please take her to the house. Now!" Renzo pleaded while the unnerving, ominous sound of the plane continued overhead. It kept circling like a vulture, spewing a barrage of machine-gun bullets, looking for prey, looking for victims, looking for death.

A line of bullets came perilously close to them, and Domenica and Adrienne accepted the reality of the situation. They ran in the direction of La Grande Maison so they could take shelter in there, if necessary, and then would continue toward the Santi home.

Just then, one of the anti-aircraft machine guns hit the bull's-eye. A cluster of bullets had found the plane's engine, which, with a sputtering sound, began a dizzying, flaming downward spiral.

There were immediate shouts of joy and praise from the remaining soldiers and villagers, all of whom had found shelter behind rocks and trees. They believed the danger was over now and had not yet realized that the plane was coming toward them like a fireball. They didn't know where it would crash but instinctively, they ran toward the entrance of La Grande Maison, seeking refuge. Suddenly, a loud, clamorous explosion was heard and felt throughout the area. The ground beneath them shook violently. The plane, still aflame, crashed right in the center of the majestic chestnut tree in the middle of the yard. Renzo scanned the area and determined that everyone was still alive and unhurt, but at the moment of impact, one of the propeller blades of the burning plane snapped off and began a violent flight of its own. He saw it bounce off the ground a couple of times and then, with a cyclone-like fury, it struck the ground just to the right of Adrienne, who had continued running and was just approaching La Grande Maison. The impact and shock of the propeller blade hitting so closely caused her knees to buckle, making her lose her balance and fall face forward to the ground. Renzo ran to her. She lay at the threshold of the entrance door, over which were written the fateful words: "Abandon hope, all ye who enter here."

When Renzo reached her, Domenica was kneeling on the ground, sobbing uncontrollably. He immediately noticed the sharp tip of the trophy poking through Adrienne's back. Turning her over, he saw she had fallen directly onto the horn, which had pierced her chest. The impact of her fall pushed it through her body. Blood was flowing profusely from her wound. She was motionless, her eyes staring emptily. Denying the obvious, Renzo called her name, but she didn't respond. He exhorted her to get up, but she didn't move. He held her wrist, hoping to find a pulse but felt nothing. He brought her hands to his lips, but her fingers—the same talented fingers that had shown such an immense dexterity at the keyboard—were hopelessly still. He passionately kissed her cheeks over and over, but the healthy, pinkish color wasn't there anymore. Her lips were not the same warm lips from which the words "*Je t'aime*" had often come. They were now cold and silent.

Renzo looked into her eyes, but his reflection was no longer there. Adrienne was dead. Renzo was petrified in horror and disbelief. He tried to speak to Adrienne but couldn't. A pair of steel hands seemed to have reached his throat and squeezed it to the point of choking him. Yet hoping that this was just a terrible nightmare, he continued to call her name and kiss the still beautiful face of that proud Corsican woman, bathing it in a river of his tears. And even though his mind, heart, and soul were enveloped in a fog of denial, he had to regrettably accept the fact that the woman he loved more than life itself, the woman who was the comfort of his soul, the woman who in the eyes of God was his wife, the woman who was to give life to their unborn child was, in fact, dead.

With that realization, an uncontrollable tremor took hold of him. He felt as if his spirit had left his flesh. Utterly terrified, he held her lifeless body tight to his heart, the trophy still imbedded in her chest, and rocked her back and forth as if she were a sleeping child. As he glanced at his surroundings, things appeared distorted, moving in slow motion, and absolutely silent. He soon saw things return to a normal pace, and it was then that he began to understand that the only bond that had ever given meaning to his life had disappeared.

Renzo's spirit had sunk to its lowest depths. He looked around and saw the weeping faces of the only people who knew their secret. Domenica knew it. Tonelli knew it, and so did Corinne. As for Padre Silvestri, Renzo suspected that he, too, knew about it, through Adrienne's visit to his confessional. And then, as he frantically stared at them, he saw through his blurry eyes the old prelate approaching, wearing on his face a benevolent, almost patronizing look of understanding. He knelt near Adrienne, alongside Renzo, made the sign of the cross, and in a soft, trembling voice began to recite a prayer in Latin, a prayer that Renzo remembered well from his days as an altar boy: the prayer for the dead.

"Through this holy oil and His own most tender mercy, may the Lord pardon you the sins you have committed. Rest in peace. Amen."

There was such a decisive finality in those words that Renzo understood he wouldn't see her smile again, nor would he ever kiss her lips. All their dreams, all their plans, all their hopes for the future vanished forever. He cursed the war, he cursed the Nazis, and he cursed Hitler and Mussolini. But all that rage brought him no relief.

He was still desperately clutching Adrienne's lifeless body when, in the stillness of the night, along with the sounds of war and the fetid, sickening smell of the burning airplane and its carbonized pilot, Renzo heard an eerie, despairing cry ring out. It was the most terrifying human scream that had ever pierced his ears.

He had no idea from where or from whom that sound was coming, and it wasn't until Padre Silvestri and the faithful Domenica shook him vigorously that he realized that it was he who, at the top of his frantic voice, was desperately calling the name of the only woman he had ever loved. "Adrienne! ... Adrienne! ... Adrienne!"

He covered her with kisses, and with his eyes floating in a lagoon of tears, he cradled her tightly in what was to be his last embrace.

24 *Leaving Corsica*

---

hree days later, on October 4, Renzo believed Adrienne had reached heaven, while he had descended to the depths of hell.

For three nights and three days, the troops fought the bloodiest battle of the Corsican campaign. The cost was heavy. Too much blood was spilled, too many young lives were lost, but to their credit, the redemption of the beleaguered Italian army had been accomplished. The mighty 90th Panzer Division was no more. At last, the intense fighting ceased. Their new enemy had been decidedly defeated. They had hammered the last nail in the Nazi coffin. American and British bomber planes sank the few ships that had dared to leave port, and all aboard died. The remaining Third Reich troops were easily captured and taken prisoner.

And lastly, together with the Allied forces, the French color troops, and the organized men of the Liberation Front, they entered the torn, almost destroyed but still unconquered city of Bastia. Their war was over. Corsica was free again and quietly had returned to being the Scented Island.

****

On the ninth of October, their exodus began. The company was one of the first to embark a small, creaking troop-transport ship at Bonifacio, headed for the port of Palau in Sardinia.

Renzo had sunk to the nadir of his life. Everything that had ever given him joy, pleasure, and peace had been taken away from him, including his reliable ambulance that, together with other equipment, had been left in Corsica to become property of the French army.

Gladly, however, Tonelli was at his side, and for a while, he was a comforting companion. But soon, completely oblivious to what he had left behind, Tonelli began to strum on his guitar, probably wondering when or where he could find another Corinne.

Renzo leaned motionless on the guardrail of the slow-moving vessel with his eyes fixed on the rugged coastline. He held the sack he had used to bring the ibex trophy to Benelli in the hospital. And as the mountain began to disappear behind them in the morning fog, resignation descended on his shoulders. He peered into the sack for one last look at what should have been a priceless memento, and then he threw it into the sea, cursing its very existence.

He knew his flesh and bones belonged to Italy. But because of Adrienne, his mind, heart, and soul would be forever linked to Corsica.